Had their lovemaking meant nothing to him?

"Look, Jo—" Jake turned"—I won't hold you to our arrangement. You were a brilliant actress with a brilliant future. Your career was interrupted, and now here's your chance to continue with it."

"You think I should take the part?" Jo asked quietly. A steady ache washed over her body. *I don't want it,* she screamed inside, *I just want to be with you. I want your love and your child....*

"It's not a case of what I think." He strode across to the window and rested his hands on the sill, and in the silence his words fell like lead. "You just have to leave, Jo. There's no point in your staying any longer."

Books by Lynsey Stevens

LYNSEY STEVENS

starting over

Harlequin Books

TORONTO • NEW YORK • LONDON
AMSTERDAM • PARIS • SYDNEY • HAMBURG
STOCKHOLM • ATHENS • TOKYO • MILAN

Harlequin Presents first edition May 1984
ISBN 0-373-10692-0

Original hardcover edition published in 1982
by Mills & Boon Limited

CHAPTER ONE

SHE had been at the cottage for a week before she saw the child. Not that it was surprising that no one had been on the beach for an entire week, as the weather couldn't have been worse. When she arrived it had been raining and it had rained fairly consistently ever since, the grey mist almost shrouding the view of the ocean.

Now she stood tensely at the plate glass window of the living-room and stared at the small figure walking along the water's edge. Occasionally the child would break into a skip and spin around or bend down to pick up a shell or a pebble and slip it carefully into a red bucket swinging in a small hand.

From this distance she was unable to tell if it was a boy child or a girl child, for the little figure was dressed in blue shorts and a white T-shirt and hat. But she didn't care. She stood and watched, wanting to tear herself away but somehow unable to do so, conscious of that same heavy weight of pain over her heart. The child sat down, oblivious, engrossed in the contents of the bucket.

The curtain fell back and she sank into the depths of a beanbag chair. Why must she be tortured in this way? She had only wanted to come down to the cottage because it was so isolated and she could be alone. It had taken some time to convince Maggie and Ben that she was now well enough to be left on her own. So what if she had had to exaggerate the truth about her reasons for wanting to be here by herself? Everything now was just a means to an end.

Maggie was convinced it would be good therapy for her to finish the novel she had started all those months ago, when life held some meaning for her. Well, she hadn't even unpacked the manuscript. She had no intention of doing so until she had to set it out to allay Maggie's suspicions.

She simply wanted to be alone, away from that world, that other yesterday world, the days of trying to go on as though her whole existence hadn't fallen apart, the days of people, of all the well-meaning friends who suggested gently that she should make a new life for herself, start over. Start over? Couldn't they understand that she had no wish, no motivation to begin again? She just wanted to be left alone.

Almost desultorily her blue-grey eyes moved slowly over the living-room, and as she fought to keep her thoughts on these more inanimate things she listened to the comforting noises of the roof materials expanding as the weak sunlight struggled further through the thinning clouds, to begin the task of drying the rain-soaked earth.

If she had still been capable of being moved by beauty this cottage would have been ideal. Built back from the beach and up a slight incline, its A-frame design sat it stoically into the green hillside. It was small, for it was only intended as a weekender, but it suited her purpose. Or at least it had up till now. Of course if the child came again she would have to leave and find somewhere else. But where?

She shook her head, bringing her thoughts back to the safety of the house. It consisted of an open covered patio overlooking the beach which led into the living-room, all rustic wood and exposed beams to the ceiling, the floorboards highly polished and covered by a couple of fluffy sheepskin rugs. A staircase went up to the only bedroom, more of an open loft, and at the back, beneath the loft, was a small kitchen, a bathroom and a tiny laundry.

Her mind fixed on the objects in her immediate

vicinity, time passed by unnoticed. In the past eighteen
months, time had developed a habit of doing that. She
could lose large pieces of her day without even noticing, but this fact didn't perturb her, because she
wanted it that way.

Eventually she stirred herself enough to recognise
that she must make an effort to eat as the light was
beginning to fade. And of course, she must begin to
prepare herself for the next day when Maggie and Ben
came down to reassure themselves that she was all
right. She knew Maggie would want to see some evi-
dence that her stay in the cottage was beneficial, other-
wise she would insist that she return home with them,
and she knew she couldn't do that.

Staying with Maggie was becoming too much of a
strain on them all. She couldn't continue leaning on
her stepsister for ever. Maggie had Ben, her husband,
and her two daughters to consider.

The strange part about it was that she didn't really
want to lean on anyone, nor did she want to stand
alone. She just wanted to exist in a warm cocoon of
emptiness where she didn't have to think, to feel. She
didn't want to look ahead and she couldn't bear to
allow herself to think back. If she began thinking about
the past she had a terrible fear that she would go
quietly insane again. And as much as life held nothing
for her she still experienced the terror of perhaps
slipping back into the black void of horror that took
her unmercifully through the whole nightmare again
and again.

Don't think! Don't think! she repeated to herself
parrot-fashion. It was the only way she could keep
herself calm. Over the months she had managed to cul-
tivate an almost mechanical mental switching off so
that she didn't have to remember that moment, a
moment that had since inflicted her with this slow
death she was experiencing.

A bell was ringing somewhere and its insistence dragged her mercilessly from sleep. She groped for the phone on her bedside table.

'Hello.'

'Jo? Jo, is that you?'

'Yes, Maggie, it's me.'

'Oh, dear, it sounds as if I've woken you up!' Maggie sounded contrite. 'Sorry about that, Jo, but I wanted to let you know that we won't be able to make it down to the cottage this weekend. Wouldn't you know it? Tracey's caught measles!'

'Oh, dear! I thought she'd had them.' Jo struggled into a sitting position.

'No. Kerry had them when she started school last year, but Tracey missed out on them then. But Jo, what about you? Are you all right down there?' Maggie asked earnestly.

'Yes, I'm fine, Maggie. It's been raining and I've had a good rest. I may ... I may get out on to the beach today,' she finished guiltily knowing full well that she had no intention of doing so.

'Oh, that's great, Jo. I'm so pleased.' Maggie's voice beamed down the line, making Jo feel even more of a fraud. 'You're not lonely, are you? Because I can leave the girls with Ben and come down on my own.'

'I'm not lonely,' Jo replied with honesty, 'so don't come down, Mag. You can't leave Tracey when she's sick. You'll only worry about her all day. I'm really enjoying it down here, it's so peaceful.'

'Well, if you're sure ...' Maggie sounded hesitant. 'Have you seen anyone around?'

'No!' Jo answered quickly. 'No. But then it has been raining.'

'I just wondered if you'd seen anyone from the O'Connor place. You know that lovely old house around the bay from the cottage that was up for sale? I pointed it out to you when we passed it last weekend.'

'No, Maggie. I've no idea if there's anyone there—I can't see it from here, can I?'

'No. It's behind a sort of rocky hill and all those trees. Oh, well, just idle curiosity. Ben and I have always liked it. I wish we could have afforded to buy it. It's beautiful, and so big! I guess we'll have to start thinking about extending the cottage. It's really too small for the family now and Dad likes to come down with us, too. Hold on, Jo.' There were muffled voices in the background. 'Are you there, Jo?'

'Yes, I'm here.'

'Ben said to tell you there've been good catches of tailor along the beaches and if you want to use his gear it's in the cupboard under the stairs. Ugh! I remember you two standing up to your waists in cold water years ago. Never could understand what fun there is in that.'

Jo could see her stepsister shuddering. 'We did enjoy it, didn't we? Thank Ben for me. I . . . I may have a try if I feel energetic,' she replied vaguely. 'I'm afraid I'm being very lazy.'

'Well, that's what you're there for, so you see that you do have a complete rest. Jo, I'd better go now, the kids are calling me. Now, are you sure you're all right?'

'Yes, Maggie, I'm sure.' Jo infused her voice with enthusiasm.

'Okay, then. All being well we'll see you next weekend. Ring me if you need anything, won't you, love? Oh, Jo? Are you still there?'

'Yes.'

'I nearly forgot. I . . . er—Jo, Aaron Daniel rang me yesterday,' Maggie finished quickly.

Instinctively Jo's hand went to the left side of her face, her fingers probing the furrowed skin from temple to jawline. 'You didn't tell him where I was, did you, Maggie?'

'No, of course not. But Jo, why not ring him up and

at least talk to him?' Maggie pleaded. 'He cared enough
to keep asking after you.'

'No, Maggie, I can't. I've finished with all that. You
told Aaron months ago. He'll . . . he'll give up eventually.'

'All right, Jo, if that's the way you want it.' Maggie
sighed. 'He's such a nice guy.' When Jo made no reply
Maggie said a hurried goodbye and hung up.

Jo put the receiver back on its cradle and sat staring
into space, her hand gently stroking her cheek, knowing each ridge of the scar, and when the pain began to
return she put her hand down to clutch the blankets.

Don't think! Don't think! she chanted the familiar
panacea. She shifted her thoughts back to Maggie and
sighed. Poor Maggie! She owed her stepsister more
than she could begin to tally up. Maggie was, had
always been, the nicest, kindest, most genuine person
Jo had ever known.

Both girls had been fifteen when Jo's mother, a
divorcee of five years, had married Maggie's father,
who had been a widower for three years. Maggie and
Jo had thought it all so romantic. Their respective
parents had been at school together and were reacquain-
ted at a school reunion. Six months later they were
married and had five happy years together before Jo's
mother's death. After her first unhappy marriage to an
alcoholic who ill-treated both his wife and his daughter, the family life Jo and her mother shared with
Maggie and her father was pure bliss.

The two girls had liked each other from their first
meeting, although no two teenagers could have been
more dissimilar. Jo was tall and fair while Maggie was
short and dark. And while Jo wanted to make acting
her career, Maggie's only ambition was to marry her
childhood sweetheart, Ben Chamberlain, and have
babies. They had both achieved what they wanted.

On her eighteenth birthday Maggie had married Ben

and could have been happier when her daughter Kerry arrived within the year, and her second daughter, Tracey, two years later.

Meanwhile, Jo had been studying drama and was beginning to be noticed in what parts she managed to get. Her parts improved, until she was given the lead in a stage play put on by a popular theatre company. That was when she met Mike and . . .

Don't think! Don't think! she almost screamed at herself. Agitated, she sprang out of bed and began to dress, telling herself to remain calm, to go quietly downstairs and fix herself a little breakfast.

Keeping her mind blank, she slowly sipped her coffee and nibbled a piece of toast, feeling the sun beginning to warm the house. Unconsciously she realised her eyes kept returning to the window of the living-room, and rather like a moth being drawn to a flame she walked across and looked down on to the beach. Her eyes raked its entire length before she admitted it was empty and she expelled the breath she was holding. The child had most probably only been visiting for the day; there was no reason why it should return. On an impulse she opened the door and stepped out on to the patio.

Three days later Jo went down on to the beach. What drove her out of the house she didn't know, but she found her bare feet luxuriating in the soft white sand before she consciously remembered thinking about it. The fine crystals were warm from the sun, had not reached the stage where they burned too hot to stand upon. She walked towards the water's edge, stopping on the hard sand, letting the water strive to touch her toes.

Once she had to step back quickly from a high wave and found herself smiling faintly. The corners of her mouth lifted upwards, taking her by surprise, her facial muscles stiff and inactive. She took a deep breath, filling her lungs with clean salty air, and smiled again, experiencing a small flicker somewhere deep within her, the nearest thing to a consciousness of living she had felt for eighteen months.

Confused by her reactions, she frowned, wondering how simply the sight of clear turquoise water could lift some of the dull weight from her body. She stood staring into the water, picking out an occasional piece of floating seaweed or a fish silverly back-lit in a wave a moment before the wave tumbled in a rush of white foam.

'Why don't you paddle your toes in the water?' came a young voice from beside her, and Jo froze, turning her head slowly in the direction of the voice, knowing instinctively who she would see, and her stomach muscles tensed until she felt nauseous.

'It's really quite warm. Not cold at all.'

The child wore the same blue shorts, coupled this time with a yellow T-shirt with Humphrey B. Bear dancing on the front. The child had one of the plainest faces Jo had seen, and as she gazed down in horror she found herself comparing this plain child with Jamie and the same anger rose to choke her, tearing mercilessly at the tentative barrier she had built so agonisingly around her heart. Why should this plain child be living while her beautiful baby was dead?

'Come on, I'll hold your hand.' Unaware of the woman's thoughts, the child took hold of her hand and gently pulled her the few steps towards the water until the shallow waves swirled about their toes.

The child giggled, a joyous, ingenuous sound that touched that same vulnerable nerve in Jo, and she felt her face pale, her mouth go suddenly dry.

'Isn't it fun?' Big blue eyes looked up at her and the child smiled widely, adding a certain piquancy to the plain little face. One small white front tooth was missing and light brown hair stuck out from beneath a towelling hat.

As Jo continued to look down at the little figure her eyes captured every detail, the long lashes fringing the dark blue eyes, the firm little chin, the way the sun had bleached the fine hair on the thin little arms, the Band-Aid stuck across one knee.

'It is fun, don't you think?' the child persisted, the smile fading a little, sensing Jo's restraint.

'Yes.' Jo found her voice. 'Yes, it is.'

Reassured, the child's smile widened again. 'My name's Sam. What's yours?'

'Jo.'

The child laughed delightedly. 'We've both got boys' names.' She wrinkled her small nose. 'I'm really Samantha but everyone calls me Sam. What's Jo short for?'

Jo hesitated. 'Joelle,' she replied slowly, reluctant to talk to this child, to anyone, but unable to turn and walk away.

'Joelle.' The child tried the sound of the name. 'That's pretty.' She gazed up objectively. 'You're pretty too. Do you wear those black glasses because the sun hurts your eyes?'

'I . . . yes. Sometimes.' She put her hand to the scarf around her hair, making sure it was still in place, holding her hair over the side of her face. She stepped backwards and the child dropped her hand. A surge of relief swept over Jo that she no longer touched the child, followed by a twinge of remorse that she was irrationally blaming this innocent child for the cruelty of fate.

'Uncle Jake does too. His eyes get very tired 'cause he stays up late at night with his books. You live up there, don't you?' One little finger pointed up at the cottage.

Jo nodded, wishing she could make the move to run back to the sanctuary of that cottage, to escape from the torture, the agony.

'I've seen you there. Do you live all alone?'

Jo nodded again. 'I . . . I'll have to get back now,' she began.

'It looks like a dolly's house, doesn't it?' continued the child. 'Uncle Jake thinks so, too. We walked along the beach one night and you had all the lights switched on and it looked like it was floating in the sky, like a magic carpet.' The big blue eyes turned back to Jo. 'We live around there, in the big house.' She pointed to the end of the bay. 'There's Uncle Jake and Chrissie and me. Uncle Jake needed to get away from the rat race.' She giggled. 'That's funny, isn't it? Rats don't race. Why are you down here all by yourself?'

'I . . . I'm on holiday.'

'Oh. It's a lovely place, isn't it? There's no one around. Uncle Jake likes it that way. People can make trouble and he doesn't want anyone coming to our place.' She looked measuringly at Joe. 'But you can. I like you, and I think Uncle Jake will like you, too, Jo,' she grinned.

Jo experienced an almost irresistible urge to throw her arms about those thin little shoulders and hug her fiercely. But of course she simply stood there trying to analyse the feelings this scrap of a child was stirring deep within her, feelings she had thought dead and buried, buried with Jamie.

What was happening to her? One minute she swung one way, and then the other. It was all going too fast, along roads she had no wish to tread again.

'I really must go now,' she said, to cover her confusion. 'I . . . There's things I have to do.'

The little girl sighed resignedly. 'Okay. Will you be coming down to the beach another day, do you suppose?' she appealed.

'I don't know. I might.' Jo chose her words carefully. 'Probably.' She took pity on the serious little face, although almost immediately she regretted her rash half-commitment.

'Great!' grinned Sam. 'Maybe we could talk again. It'll be fun having someone else to talk to. I mean, Chrissie's usually busy and Uncle Jake spends lots of time on his books. Do you think you might come down tomorrow?' Her big eyes opened questioningly.

'Well, perhaps. If I have time.' Jo forced herself to step away. 'Goodbye.'

' 'Bye, Jo.' A small hand was lifted in a wave. 'I'll see you another day.'

When she reached the patio Jo turned to look back at the beach. The child still stood where she had left her and the small arm rose again in an energetic wave.

For the next two days the child walked along the beach and sat watching the cottage for a time before moving slowly on, stopping every now and then to check that Jo hadn't appeared. Jo stood back from the living-room window, unable to go down to the child although she knew deep down she wanted to do just that.

On the third day Maggie rang again in a fever of agitation to say that Ben had unbelievably caught the measles from his daughter, so their trip down to the cottage had to be put off once more. Perhaps it was the thought of being alone again for another week, but when the child appeared on the beach Jo went out of the house before allowing herself to think about going or staying, and she was halfway down the grassy bank before the child saw her. Jumping to her feet, she quickly dusted the sand from the back of her shorts and ran across the beach.

'Hi, Jo!' The little face beamed happily. 'I thought you were never ever going to come down here again. I thought perhaps I'd dreamed you.'

Jo's face tried a smile again, which seemed to please

the child, and they began walking slowly towards the water.

'Uncle Jake came back yesterday,' Sam chatted gaily. 'He went up to town and he bought me a surprise. Guess what it was?'

'I couldn't begin to imagine.'

'I'll give you a clue. It's something you can eat.' Sam popped one finger in her mouth.

'A chocolate?'

'No. But you're really close. Want me to tell you?' Jo nodded.

'A lollipop. It was round and red and white stripes and nine inches long—I measured it with my ruler. I've still got some left. Would you like me to bring you some tomorrow?' Sam asked.

'Oh, no. No, you keep it for yourself. It was nice of your uncle to bring it for you, wasn't it?'

Sam nodded. 'Uncle Jake's wonderful. You know, if I was old enough I'd marry Uncle Jake,' she said seriously. 'I really would.'

'You'll have to tell him that,' Joe smiled again.

'I did.' Sam frowned. 'Lexie laughed at me and said I'd have to wait in line.' She looked up at Jo. 'I don't like Lexie. I never know what she's talking about, and besides, she doesn't like me.'

At a loss about handling this confidence Jo paused before attempting a comment and the little girl continued.

'I heard her tell Uncle Jake I was the plainest Jane she'd ever seen.' Sam kicked the sand with one bare foot. 'I hope she goes away.'

'Maybe you misunderstood her,' Jo began, remembering her first impressions of the child and knowing a moment of guilty remorse.

Sam shrugged her thin shoulders. 'Let's sit down here on the sand, Jo.' She threw herself down and patted the spot beside her.

When Jo had lowered herself on to the sand Sam rested her arms on her raised knees and put her firm little chin on her hands. 'I wish you could meet Lexie so you could tell me if you think she's pretty, Jo. Uncle Jake thinks so, I guess. She's his fi ... er ... fi ...' she sighed, 'you know, they're engaged. At least, I think they are.'

'His fiancée,' Jo finished, and Sam nodded.

'I wouldn't mind her so much, Jo, but when Uncle Jake's there she's really nice to me. But when he's not there she's awful. I don't think I want to have her live with us. I just know she'll ...' Sam stopped, and Jo turned to look at her.

The little girl glanced down at the sand and then back to Jo. 'She'll make me have the light off when I go to bed,' she said in a rush, and the naked fear in the blue eyes brought a rush of recognition and then understanding from Jo.

'I hate the dark except when Uncle Jake's with me,' said the little girl softly.

'I used to be afraid of the dark, too,' said Jo, almost to herself, and they both sat in silence for a few minutes.

'Chrissie's been cooking Uncle Jake's favourite dinner for tonight. He loves shepherd's pie,' Sam's eyes grew large, 'and we're having a pavlova for dessert, a passionfruit one.'

'That sounds delicious.'

'Hey, would you like to come over for dinner?' Sam beamed excitedly.

'Oh, no, Sam, I don't think I could. And I somehow think your uncle might be a little annoyed if you just invited a stranger to dinner.' Jo smiled, wondering how this uncle, this paragon of virtue, of Sam's would handle such a situation, and she chuckled. The noise rose within her and came out like music to her ears. She had actually laughed! A week ago she had thought she would never smile again, and she owed it to this child who had drawn from her an initial hatred.

'I could go and ask him now?'

'No, it's all right, Sam. I'll be quite busy tonight,' Jo said hurriedly.

'What will you be doing?'

Before Jo could answer a voice calling the child's name broke the tranquillity of the seascape and they both stood up, instinctively turning towards the voice. The little girl smiled expectantly, but Jo was not aware of it. She stood transfixed, a thousand of the old fears crowding in on her, holding her immobile.

As the figure approached at what seemed like an alarmingly superhuman speed Jo took in the fact that he was tall, suntanned, very muscular and quite dark-haired. The only clothing he wore was a pair of ancient denim shorts, frayed at the edges as though they had once been jeans and were now cut off mid-thigh. The legs of the shorts hugged those muscular thighs and the beltless waist was slung low on his hips.

The fact that he was obviously very fit recorded itself somewhere in Jo's subconscious. Her heart began to flutter wildly in her breast like a bird trapped in a cage and her hand went shakily to ensure that her scarf was in place. She had to get away before this magnificent animal came too close. He belonged to that other world of beautiful people, that other time of . . . But her legs refused to move, had begun to quiver uselessly.

Now that he was closer Jo could pick out his features, the dark eyes, the chiselled planes of his high cheekbones and square jaw, the full curve of his lips, the peppering of grey in his dark hair as it was neatly shaped over his ears, a few front strands lifting in the breeze. It was a handsome face, but now they could see the dark scowl on his brow. The little girl's smile faded.

'Sam, you'd better go home. Chrissie's been looking for you,' he said tersely, and those dark eyes went from his niece to Jo, spearing her with their flinty sharpness.

'I've been talking, Uncle Jake . . .' Sam began.

'All right, head off home. I'll catch up with you,' he said, his tone softening a little.

'Okay, Uncle Jake. See you, Jo,' Sam said quietly, and sketched a small wave before she set off along the beach.

Neither of them made any attempt to say anything until the child was out of earshot. Six feet of hard sand separated them and the current of electricity that bridged that distance filled Jo with a sudden inexplicable terror. She recognised her own vibes as fear, but his were much more involved, more complex, although she sensed that a cold anger seemed the overriding emotion. The colour left her face and, turning on one foot, she raced towards the cottage.

The soft sand impeded her progress, straining the muscles of her legs, and her breathing became laboured. She set her sights on the grassy bank. If she could only reach . . . A hand came out from behind her, none too gently grabbing her arm. She came to a halt, almost fell, as he swung her effortlessly around, steadying her, as she tried to catch her breath.

'Not so fast, you beautiful little bitch,' he said.

'Let me go!' Her voice came out huskily, uneven. 'You let me go!'

'Not before we talk.'

'I don't . . . I don't want to talk to you, Let me go!'

'Oh, we'll talk all right. At least, I intend to talk to you, and I intend you to listen. Now hear this, Miss Whoever-you-are. You can take yourself back stat to wherever or whatever newspaper, magazine or scandal sheet that sent you here, and if you print one word about my niece or myself I swear I'll sue you for every penny you expect to make in your lifetime!' His eyes

bored holes in hers, smouldering with his barely controlled anger.

'What ... what are you talking about?' Jo's knees
began to tremble again and it occurred to her that he
might be slightly deranged.

'You're not dealing with an innocent child now, so
you can come clean.' He gave a harsh laugh. 'Make no
mistake, I mean what I say. One word and I'll break
you and whoever you work for.'

'You're mad! Let me go!' Jo's struggles were no
match for him. He held her completely at his mercy
and as she struggled he pulled her against him, her
hand finding the hardness of his bare chest. The thin
material of her skirt could not disguise the hardness of
his thighs pressed against hers.

His skin was hot from the sun, with only a light
covering of hair for one so dark, and her eyes moved
upwards, following the firm column of his throat, the
aggressive thrust of his jaw, moving quickly over his
lips to his eyes. She saw now that they were dark blue and
fringed by dark lashes as long as her own, and a feeling
long forgotten began to stir, tingling her nerve ends.

Her lips trembled as his attention focused on them,
remained on their perfect shape, and the expression
in the dark blue depths of his eyes changed minutely.
His head came down and his lips claimed hers, taking
her completely by surprise, moving masterfully, so that
beneath that mastery she was pliant, ductile, before
she was aware of her surrender.

Jo's senses swung in limbo. Her body responded as
she suspected he knew it would, her lips moving beneath his, and she tasted the salt on them. Her hand
curled against the steady thump of his heartbeat. But
her mind was a thing apart, that stood back and looked
on with a feeling akin to revulsion. What kind of
woman was she? Hadn't she kissed another man in just
this same way? Hadn't she allowed him to caress her?

To possess her? To be his until death . . .

She pushed away from him in self-disgust, her breast heaving as she fought to get herself back under control. His own breathing seemed a little fast as well, but his face bore no change of expression.

He laughed then, that same harsh laugh, and cold shivers ran up her spine. 'You know, maybe you played your cards all wrongly. If you'd come to me and asked me personally I might have given you official permission. I'm sure we could have worked things out,' he smiled at that, leaving her under no misapprehension about his meaning. 'I've got an eye for a pretty face— what man hasn't?—and what I can see of yours more than passes muster. Why cover it up? Let's have a look at the rest of it.'

His hand moved and removed her sunglasses. Jo strained against his hold, hysteria rising within her like bile. She had to stop him.

'No!' she almost sobbed. 'No. Please, don't!' Fear added strength to her fight to free herself and she twisted her head back from his relentless hand. Through her terror she heard him laugh again, and then he had his hand on the scarf and it was coming away from her face.

Her hair fell forward in a cascade of blonde waves. It had always been her best feature, she had been told. And it still was, was the one thing not spoiled. Naturally honey-blonde, it fell shoulder-length in a swirl of sunlit fluid gold.

She turned her face away, her lips trembling, her eyes downcast from the unaccustomed glare, and heard him catch his breath.

'Well, well. There lurked a ravishing beauty,' he said softly, his fingers taking hold of her chin. 'Why hide such exquisiteness behind that disguise?' he asked, and pulled her face around so that she was looking straight at him.

Her blue-grey eyes watched him now with resignation. All the fight had at that moment left her body and as his eyes moved slowly, appreciatively over each feature the sea wind gave a slightly stronger gust, and with apparent cruel amusement lifted her hair back from her face.

She didn't even attempt to raise her hand to hide it but watched him for the dawning of horror, knowing it would come as it always did. The dead weight was back upon her body and she felt herself turn suddenly numbingly cold.

It appeared to Jo that his eyes went in slow motion to the rend of the scar down her cheek. One minute his eyes held a cruel sort of teasing mixed with a reluctant admiration and then she knew he was exercising admirable self-control in stopping himself from flinching, the muscles of his jaw tensing.

With a calm detachment she had to admit that he took it rather well, better than most; and when she felt the slackening of his hold on her arm she firmly detached herself and turned towards the cottage, taking one or two slow steps before she broke into an almost frenzied race away from him, to the sanctuary of the cottage. Away from him, from all the memories his first admiring glance evoked.

But she needn't have run up the slope, or slammed and locked the door behind her, because he made no attempt to follow her. When she had caught her breath and moved stumbling across to the window the beach was completely empty.

CHAPTER TWO

THAT night the nightmares returned to taunt her. She remained awake for hours into the night holding desperately on to consciousness, even though an angry dark face swam before her eyes defying all her efforts to wipe him from her mind.

The scene on the beach replayed itself over and over as she lay tossing on her hot sheets. He obviously thought she was some sort of journalist. But why? Who was he, that he expected a reporter to go to any lengths to get a story about him? She didn't even know his name. Only Jake. Jake who? It wasn't a common name. And his face wasn't familiar. She hadn't seen him before.

But perhaps she had seen him and she'd forgotten. Since the accident she was quite often not positive about a lot of things—incidents, people, places, especially things that had occurred just before the accident. But she would have remembered him. Wouldn't she?

His face materialised in her mind's eye once again and that same tremor passed over her body. Her hand went to her lips as she again experienced the pressure, the sensations of his mouth moving down to claim hers.

No! she cried inside. No! She never wanted that closeness again. The oneness. The joy. The disillusionment. The pain of losing. Don't think! she began to repeat to herself over and over.

Eventually she slept, and the nightmare came just as she knew it would. When it began she tried unsuccessfully to wake herself so that she would escape the agony she knew would come, but with an unrelenting lack of mercy the chord was struck in her subconscious and the whole tragedy began to play itself through, from its unsuspecting beginning to its horrifying end.

It was the utter blackness of the night that filled those hours before the accident occurred, that and Mike's ill-humour, Jamie's fretfulness, her own disquiet. In truth they should never have been on that road that night, but they had missed their way in the unfamiliar area, and, after reaching a battered signpost, they had taken what, according to their road map, was a short cut back on to the main road they should have taken in the beginning.

The small argument she had had with Mike at the crossroads came back to accuse her, ballooning out of all proportion. In his safety seat in the back of the car Jamie had whimpered, adding to the atmosphere between his parents. However, finally Jo had soothed him to sleep and they pushed on in a strained, exasperated silence.

When the road passed from narrow bitumen to rough gravel as it wound up through the rain-forest Jo had suggested nervously that they turn back, only to have Mike angrily remind her that it was only ten kilometres to the highway via this road. Turning back would take them an extra sixty kilometres.

The side of the road fell steeply away into the blackness of the trees and she had moved instinctively closer to Mike, slackening her seat-belt a little. Almost every night since she found her memory slowly returning she had lived through the horror of the next few seconds. Just seconds, that was all it took to wipe away all she held precious in her life. For months afterwards she had lain in her white hospital bed holding any memories of that night buried deep in her subconscious, not permitting herself to think about it.

Some suggested to her that it was the hand of fate, others the will of God, that took over at that time, but coincidence accepted its cue and saved a life. In her feverish agony Jo begged to know why. Why save her for this half life, her face disfigured? And why did Jamie, so innocent . . .?

As Mike swung the car up and around a right-hand curve Jamie woke up with a start, his favourite toy, a much worn teddy bear, slipping from his grasp, and he cried tiredly for Jo to pick it up for him. She unclipped her seat-belt and, as she leant over to retrieve the bear, a car coming down the mountain sped widely around the sharp turn. The two vehicles glanced off each other with a rending of tearing steel. The oncoming car spun around, smashing front-on into the solid rocky hillside, killing the driver intantly.

Unable to control their car, Mike fought to keep it on the road, but it slithered over the soft verge. As it disappeared over the edge Jo was thrown clear, while Mike and Jamie tumbled in the car, down through the trees.

She lay unconscious for hours, and in the grip of the nightmare she lived again those moments when she opened her eyes to the blackness, to the steady drizzle of the misty rain that was falling, to the paralysing terror of not knowing where she was, who she was, or how she came to be lying on the damp musty earth. A thousand mind-snapping horrors surged inside her head in those first few seconds.

She knew she thought she had lost her sight and when she went to climb to her feet, to escape, her numbed body refused to move and she was sure she was paralysed. She screamed in her sleep, and the sound struck a sensitive chord in her memory, bringing back the same surge of hysteria, before the welcome blackness returned.

Her next recollections were of crawling over the edge of the slope on to the roughness of the gravel road, not knowing how she came to be there or how long it had taken her to reach the top. Her injuries were quite extensive, her right arm was badly broken, her ribs were cracked, her spleen ruptured, and the left side of her face was slashed open by a dead branch at the bottom of the tree that had halted her fall down the slope. But she recalled feeling no pain. Her whole body was numb—or perhaps her mind had reached the limit of its endurance and had simply switched off.

Later they discovered she had slowly crawled on her stomach up the slope from about a hundred feet down. She must have recognised the road as such, for she was able to climb to her feet, and she began to follow it down, because it seemed lighter and she could make out the outlines of some of the trees.

Even so she almost walked into the car before she saw it. Feeling her way carefully around it, she found the driver's side door and tried unsuccessfully to pull it open. As she put her hand through the open window her fingers encountered the still form of the driver slumped forward over the wheel. Another scream rose within her as some instinctive sense told her he was dead.

She could hear herself babbling incoherently as she tried the handle again. Leaving it, she moved to the back door, almost falling over as it swung outwards. Feverishly she groped all over the back seat, finding nothing, not understanding the agitated sobbing that broke from her, knowing only that she was experiencing some huge loss. Backing away from the dark outline of the crashed car, she ran sobbing, her physical pain meaning nothing as another more frightful agony racked her body, more terrible in that its full significance eluded her tormented thoughts.

The sun was beginning to light the horizon when a rather ancient utility came rattling along the road and slithered to a jarring halt in front of her. The figure she presented, swaying in the middle of the rarely used road, must have given the driver the fright of his life. Ted Marsden. She remembered his name even now, saw his concerned weather beaten face as he stumbled from his truck to catch her as she began to crumple up. She remembered nothing of him lifting her into the truck and racing her back to his farmhouse where his wife began to dress her wounds while he rang for the ambulance and the police.

As though she was hovering above herself Jo could hear the Marsdens talking, wondering what had happened to get her into that state. She was unaware that her clothing was torn, wet and filthy, that the blood from the slash on her face had matted her hair, covered her arm and chest, that her broken arm hung crookedly and that she muttered constantly about what sounded like 'the back seat'. And although she remembered nothing of the high-speed dash by ambulance she was already in hospital by the time the police found the crashed car and realised from the gouges in the shoulder of the road and the trail of broken trees down the hillside that another vehicle had gone over the side of the mountain.

Jo was suffering from temporary amnesia and it was a month before Maggie gently told her that Mike and Jamie had been killed instantly that night. By then large pieces of her life were coming back to her, but for two weeks she assured Maggie that she knew no one by the name of Mike or Jamie. Just as it was a battered toy teddy bear that had saved her life, so it was a teddy bear that had pushed her that last step over the line of sanity.

She was in a private room and only Maggie and Ben were allowed to see her. She even became agitated when a different nurse entered her room. One day as she sat up in bed, her face still bandaged, her arm in plaster, her ribs still painful, the door opened and a woman peeped in. Seeing Jo, she quickly apologised for having chosen the wrong room, but Jo didn't hear a word the woman said. Her eyes were fixed on the child at the woman's side, a child clutching a small teddy bear in one hand.

All the missing pieces fell agonisingly into place, flashing before her like rapier thrusts—meeting Mike, her long white dress, the church and the confetti, laughter. Another hospital bed and a pink little cherub in her arms, a toddler with huge blue eyes and soft golden curls. And the rending screech of dashing metal as she reached over for a faded yellow teddy bear.

Her scream brought nurses from everywhere, and even as the sedative she was given began to work her hoarse throat called for Mike to get Jamie out of the car, and dwindled to a brokenhearted cry for her lost child.

Jo woke herself sobbing, and as her swollen red-rimmed eyes registered the light of dawn she realised her sheets and pillow were wet, her body bathed in perspiration. It was almost three months since she had suffered through that nightmare. She had been beginning to think it was all safely behind her, that she had strengthened her mind to holding it at bay.

It seemed now that she was wrong, and she felt herself begin to shake. Was she going to have to suffer it for the rest of her life? Did she have to wait for an incident such as that one on the beach to trigger off the whole terrible ordeal again? She squeezed her eyes tightly shut. Oh, God, just let me be! Please don't let it all start again!

CHAPTER THREE

FOR the next few days Jo rarely ate or slept. Dark circles appeared beneath her eyes and her cheekbones began to grow prominent in her face, making her look ill and drawn, although she was totally unaware of her appearance.

She returned to her old occupation of sitting for hours staring at nothing, thinking about nothing. Somewhere in the back of her mind, like a faint flicker of a failing light, she knew she had to make an effort to climb out of her depression before it took too substantial a hold, pulling her back to those dreadful months when she had been lost in the black void of nothingness.

If she stood up she could ring Maggie. Maggie would come down right away. Maggie would talk to her, bring her round. Maggie would know what to do.

But no! She must learn to do it on her own, independent of Maggie, use her own resources, her own store of willpower. What willpower? she chastised herself. With a spurt of her old determination she forced herself out of the chair and into the kitchen. Without stopping to think she put on the water to boil and set out the teapot and a cup and saucer.

While she waited for the tea to brew she found her hairbrush and began to brush her hair, letting it fall freely about her face, keeping in her mind the picture of the face she used to have, the glossy studio portrait that appeared in movie magazines and television weeklies, a face unravaged by a gaping, savage rend . . .

Don't think! Don't think! her reflexes began to

chant, and she turned back to the teapot. Her teacup
was in her hand, the hot strong aroma teasing her
suddenly empty stomach, making her realise she was
hungry, when a soft tapping sound held her motionless.
Someone was knocking at the front door.

Maggie! Jo took a step forward and then stopped.
No, Maggie would phone first. She drew a sharp
breath. He wouldn't come up here, would he? No. No,
the tap was too light. He would be far more aggressive
in his approach.

'Jo? Jo? Are you home?' came a little voice. 'It's
Sam.'

Setting her cup on the breakfast bar, Jo walked
across to the door and slowly unlocked it to face the
child.

'Hello, Jo.' A worried frown sat on the child's brow
and she stood on one foot and then the other. 'Are you
well?'

'Yes, Sam, I'm . . . I'm fine,' Jo replied hesitantly.

The child took her hand from behind her back and
proffered a brown paper bag. 'Uncle Jake sent this
back. It's your scarf and your glasses, from the other
day. Uncle Jake said he was sorry you left without
them.'

Jo stared at the packet before taking it from the small
hand. 'Thank you.'

'It's okay.' Sam's head turned to one side, her eyes
questioning, but she asked nothing. 'There's a letter in
the bag as well for you to read, from Uncle Jake. I
asked him to write it.' She spoke at last.

Jo held the bag as though it was likely to explode
any minute, her mind making guesses at the contents
of any note that revolting man could have written,
wanting to throw the bag as far as she could.

'Aren't you going to open it?' Sam asked.

'Yes, of course. You'd better come on in.' Jo stood
back and the child stepped inside, eyes wide as she

gazed about her. 'I was about to have a cup of tea. Would you like a cold drink? Some milk?'

'I'd like some tea, too,' the child smiled. 'I have a cup of tea with Chrissie sometimes.' She watched while Jo poured it out before she climbed up on to the stool at the breakfast bar. 'Uncle Jake drinks coffee.'

Jo sat opposite the child, her eyes on the brown paper bag lying on the bench top by her hand. She might as well get it over with. Resolutely she opened the bag, conscious of the child's eyes on her. The sheet of paper was folded once and she opened it out. The first three words were like a blow to the solar plexus, restricting her lungs, making her feel faint. She caught her trembling lip with her teeth to stop their chatter. 'Dear Miss Brent.' So he knew who she was.

'Dear Miss Brent, My niece would like you to have dinner with her this evening at six-thirty. If you have no transport my housekeeper, Mrs Christiansen, will collect you. Unfortunately I shall be tied up in the city and don't expect to be back.' It was signed J. Marshall.

'Will you please come, Jo?' Sam's voice cut into her thoughts and she turned from the bold handwriting to the child. 'Chrissie's a very good cook. I've asked her to make you a passionfruit pavlova. Remember I was telling you about pavlovas?'

'I don't know, Sam. I don't go out much. I've been ill and . . .' she began, and the child's face fell. 'I suppose if I wasn't late I could come.' The words tumbled out of her mouth before she could bite them back, and then it was too late.

'That's great!' Sam's face lit up with the shining smile Jo remembered from the beach and the child slid off the stool and ran around to unselfconsciously wind her thin little arms around Jo's waist.

'We'll have such fun. I can show you Snuffy—he's my kitten. And Betsy, my doll, and all my toys. Do you suppose we would have time to read a story?' she chattered, unaware of the tumult of emotions warring inside Jo. 'My mummy used to read me stories.'

Initially, as the child touched her, Jo had frozen, but her arms had moved instinctively about the child's body. Somehow Sam was on her knee and a sob caught in Jo's throat at the remembered feel of the soft body, the smell of clean soft hair. A tear trickled on to Jo's cheek and the child's face was all concern.

'What's the matter, Jo? Is it because of your sore face?' Her brows drew together, blue eyes filled with an almost adult compassion. 'Uncle Jake said you'd hurt your face. Does it hurt very much?'

'No.' Jo found her voice. 'No, it doesn't hurt.'

Sam's hand went up to touch Jo's hair, moving it back, and then the little fingers gently ran over the raised flesh. 'How did it get there?' she asked.

Never before since her accident had anyone touched that side of her face. Only Jo's own fingers had followed the jagged trail down her cheek, and she sat immobile as the child moved a finger over it. And she experienced none of the emotions she thought she should be feeling. Jo's fingers covered the child's, holding the little fingers, wanting to pull the child fiercely to her.

'It was a car accident,' she said at last.

Sam nodded. 'Oh. Can't the doctor fix it?'

Jo shook her head. 'No. I have to get used to it being a part of me,' she said absently, recalling Maggie saying just that. 'If you won't let them operate, Jo, you'll have to get used to it being a part of you.'

'You can hardly see it, Jo. It's behind your hair,' Sam told her, patting her sympathetically on the arm, 'so please don't cry about it. You're still the prettiest lady I've ever seen.'

'Oh, Sam!' Jo's voice broke and she hugged the child to her, the bittersweet pleasure an agony in itself. How often had she clutched Jamie to her the way she was holding this child, soothed him, loved him, poured out on his soft little body all the feelings a mother felt for her child, all the tenderness that she and Mike seemed to have misplaced somewhere along the way.

With just a tiny bit of imagination she could almost allow herself to believe that this plain little scrap was actually Jamie, Jamie with his blond curls and bright blue eyes and engaging grin. She pulled herself up as her stomach churned nauseously. Jamie was dead and nothing, no one could bring him back. Not even this innocent child who had no part in what had gone before. Firmly Jo released the child's arms from around her neck. 'Our tea will be cold if we don't drink it,' she said huskily, and looked away from the clear innocence of the child's eyes. 'I may . . . I think I have some biscuits somewhere here.' She opened a tin and offered it to Sam.

'Thank you.' The little girl deliberated before making her choice and smiling up at Jo. 'Are you having one too?'

'No. No, thanks.'

'Are you going to write a letter back to Uncle Jake?' Sam asked after she had eaten two biscuits and sipped her tea with all the air of a grown-up.

'I suppose I should.' Jo fetched her pen and a spare piece of typing paper from the small table where she'd stacked her manuscript. Sitting back at the breakfast bar opposite the child, she stared down blankly at the pen in her hand as it hovered over the rectangle of paper. Her heart was skipping and Jake Marshall's tense face swam before her. When, in the vividness of her memory, his expression went from anger to appreciation she blinked quickly trying to dispel the image and settle her quivering nerves.

'Can't you think of what to say?' Sam's voice cut across her fancies and Jo looked up into the child's enquiring face. 'Uncle Jake took ages to write his letter to you, too. He frowned like this.' Sam furrowed her brow.

Jo smiled faintly and took a deep breath.

'Dear Mr Marshall,' she wrote, her fingers feeling stiff and unused to wielding a pen, 'I will be pleased to have dinner with your niece. I have my own transport. Thank you.'

She deliberated over her signature, nibbling the end of the pen, wishing he hadn't recognised her. Such was the power of advertising, she thought wryly. It was fully two years since her last assignment and yet Jake Marshall had not forgotten the face that had sold millions of dollars' worth of a well known complexion soap.

Eventually she scrawled 'J. Harrison' beneath the couple of lines of writing. Perhaps he would think he was mistaken, that she couldn't be Joelle Brent, ex-model. Ex-actress. Ex-wife. Ex-mother. Ex everything. Her hand shook slightly as she folded the sheet of paper over and handed it across to the child.

Sam put it carefully in the pocket of her jeans and smiled up at Jo. 'Well, I'd better go now.' She took a last sip of her tea. 'Uncle Jake said I wasn't to be long because he's leaving for the city.' She slid off the stool and skipped across to the door, turning back to Jo before she went out. 'He's probably going to see Lexie.' She wrinkled her small nose. 'Chrissie says men like to go out with ladies every so often. Do you think that's right, Jo?' she asked gravely, her head to one side.

'I guess it is,' Jo replied carefully.

'Then why doesn't Uncle Jake take me and Chrissie out instead of Lexie?' She raised her small hands. 'Lexie's horrible!'

'Now, Sam, I don't think that's a very nice thing to say,' Jo began, and Sam sighed loudly.

'I s'pose not. It's rude, isn't it? But Uncle Jake's so wonderful. He's nice—like you are, Jo,' she smiled and lifted her hand to wave. 'See you tonight!' And she was gone.

The light was fading by the time Jo climbed into her very ancient Mini and she gave the few grey clouds in the sky a cursory glance as she fitted the key into the ignition and switched it on. She had to press the starter a number of times before the engine reluctantly fired, and it spluttered its displeasure at being backed up the rather steep driveway to the narrow bitumen road that fringed the hill coastline.

However, the car settled down as she drove slowly around to the house where Sam lived, the old O'Connor place, as Maggie called it. She hoped Maggie didn't ring while she was out and become worried when Jo failed to answer. Her own call to her stepsister about half an hour ago had rung out, so Maggie was most probably visiting Ben's parents.

A flutter began in the pit of her stomach as she turned down the long driveway and drew the car to a halt at the back of a large rambling house which appeared to have a wide verandah running around the three visible sides. The garden ran riot here behind the house sheltered from the sea winds by the building. As she closed the door of the car Sam came running across the grass and threw her arms around Jo's waist. She was dressed in the inevitable faded jeans and T-shirt with a blue windcheater as some deference to the chilly breeze.

'Hi! Gee, it's great you're here, Jo.' Sam slipped her small hand into Jo's. 'You know, you're my very first friend I've ever had to dinner.'

'I'm ... I'm looking forward to it too,' Jo replied haltingly. 'I ... I haven't been out to dinner for quite some time.'

Sam beamed happily as she led Jo up the few steps

on to the verandah. A short little bird of a woman came rushing out through the open doorway, her thin grey hair escaping in wisps from the carelessly fixed bun at the back of her head. Face wreathed in smiles, she wiped her hands on her apron and shook Jo's hand eagerly.

'Chrissie, this is my friend Jo,' Sam said proudly.

'How do you do, Jo. I'm Joan Christiansen,' laughed the older woman.

'Joelle Harrison, Mrs Christiansen.' Jo smiled back, again registering the perceptible stiffness of her facial muscles as the corners of her mouth rose, her hand going nervously to check that her hair still fell over the scar on her cheek.

'Call me Chrissie—everyone does. And I'll call you Jo if I may.' She smiled down at the little girl her hand gently patting the child's cheek. 'Sam talks about you so much I doubt I could call you anything else!'

They stepped into a small vestibule which had a hallway running off to the right obviously leading to the bedrooms while a large pot plant stand screened the dining room and kitchen on the left. Straight ahead was the open living-room with huge plate glass windows that afforded a panoramic view of the beach.

'Dinner won't be more than a few minutes,' said Chrissie. 'Take Jo into the living-room, Sam love, and I'll call you when it's ready.'

Jo placed her bag and the light jacket she had brought with her on one of the comfortable old lounge chairs and crossed to gaze out at the view. Although darkness had just about fallen she could still see the pearly sheen on the water and the lightness of the expanse of sandy beach. The patch of dark blackness to the left was the grove of windblown shrubs that grew before the rocky outcrop which effectively shielded the house from her view from the cottage.

'It's pretty, isn't it?' asked Sam, kneeling on the arm of a lounge chair so that she could follow Jo's gaze.

'Yes, beautiful.' Jo sighed and turned to look at the child. 'Have you been here long?'

Sam's plain little face seemed to pale before Jo's eyes and a flicker of fear touched the blue eyes, making them appear large and round in the thinness of her face.

'Ages.' She pulled at the binding on the lounge chair. 'Uncle Jake brought me to live with him and we've been to lots of places. But I like this place best of all.'

'Well, it's a very nice place to live.' Jo made her voice light and the child seemed to relax.

'Mmm. I love playing on the beach. But I'd love to have someone to play with.' Sam sighed loudly. 'Sometimes Uncle Jake comes down to make sand-castles with me, but he's very busy with his books.' The wide smile lit her face again. 'It's great having you to talk to now, Jo, and Uncle Jake says it's all right for me to talk to you, but I already knew it would be before he even said so. Would you like to come and see my room? And I can show you my toys. There's Betsy and Tubby and . . .' She had hold of Jo's hand to lead her away when Chrissie joined them.

'Dinner's ready, so you'll have to postpone your sightseeing and the introductions until after we've eaten, love.'

By the time Chrissie brought out her highly recommended pavlova Jo suddenly realised she was genuinely enjoying herself. She was more relaxed than she had been for ages. Her hand hadn't found the rough edges of the scar all evening, and the thought made her feel almost lightheaded. Perhaps she was taking the first tentative steps to being in command of herself again? Being whole once more? Starting over . . .

Chrissie asked no personal questions during their meal and if Sam's topic of conversation seemed to run along the same track, her Uncle Jake, then Jo was even beginning to accept the mention of his name without experiencing that tiny twist of unease in the pit of her stomach.

After dinner Jo insisted on helping with the dishes while Sam very importantly stacked everything carefully away. Then she spent an hour or so with the little girl meeting her kitten and all her dolls and stuffed animals, seeing all her treasures. At nine o'clock Chrissie decided it was time for Sam to change into her pyjamas and climb into bed.

'Will you read me a story, Jo?' Sam asked as she settled back against her pillow, her eyes large and bright.

'Now, Sam, Jo may be tired of dancing attendance on you,' began Chrissie.

'Oh, no, that's not it at all,' Jo hastened to reassure the little girl as her face fell. 'I just don't want to make your night too late.'

Sam grinned and pulled a tattered book out of the small bookshelf built into the head of her bed. 'Oh, Uncle Jake said I could have a late night tonight seeing as it's special 'cause you were coming, Jo.' She quickly found the story she was looking for and handed the book to Jo. 'It's my favourite—*The Happy Prince.*' She sighed and wriggled down into the bed.

'I'll go and make us a nice cup of tea, Jo,' said Chrissie quietly. 'When you've finished the story you can leave the reading lamp on for Sam until she goes to sleep and just come through to the kitchen.'

By the time Jo had finished the sad little story Sam's eyelids were drooping and she sleepily wound her thin little arms around Jo's neck and nuzzled into her shoulder. 'That was lovely, Jo. Thank you for reading it to me.'

A wild rush of feelings, half pleasure, half pain, gathered deep within Jo and she closed her eyes to ward it off, holding the child against her, forcing herself, begging herself, not to think about Jamie. But a tear escaped and trickled down her cheek to fall on Sam's arm. The child looked up at Jo with a worried frown and Jo quickly dashed the tear away.

'Don't cry, Jo.' Sam patted her arm sympathetically. 'When I cried over *The Happy Prince* Uncle Jake said not to be sad because it means that love goes on for ever and ever, even when you're far apart.'

Jo gathered the child to her and then tucked the sheets around her and with a whispered goodnight almost bolted for the door. In the hallway she sagged against the wall, clutching at the cool paintwork to stop herself sinking to the floor.

What a fool she'd been to come here! She should have known better. The child brought it all streaming back, and that was what she feared the most, to be reminded, to reveal to her all that she had lost.

Her hand went to her cheek, her fingers finding the jagged scar. Her face was something she could learn to live with in time. But to live without Jamie. She couldn't . . . Don't think! Don't think! she repeated in her head, dragging great steadying gulps of air into her lungs. Wearily she stood away from the support of the wall and made herself take a few faltering steps forward. She must get away, go back to the cottage.

'Ah, there you are, Jo.' Chrissie came towards her. 'Come and have that cup of tea.'

'Well, I . . . It's late,' Jo stammered. 'I think perhaps I should be getting home.'

'Better wait a little, dear, it's teeming outside, you'd be soaked just running to your car,' said Chrissie.

Jo then realised that the drumming noise was not inside her head but the sound of the rain on the aluminium tiled roof.

'Such a pity the weather's bad. Rain down here at the coast is so depressing.' Chrissie led the way back to the kitchen with Jo following reluctantly behind.

'However, the forecast is for it to clear by tomorrow. Now, how do you like your tea?'

'White, please.' Jo sat down. 'Without sugar.'

Chrissie poured the tea and passed Jo her cup. 'There we are. You do look a trifle pale, Jo. Aren't you feeling well?'

'No, I'm fine. Just tired, I guess,' Jo replied, warming her cold hands on the hot teacup.

Chrissie clucked soothingly. 'I hope Sam hasn't made you tired. You know, if she becomes too much for you, you just say so and I'll have a talk to her. Jake wouldn't care for her to be making a nuisance of herself.'

'Oh, she's no bother. I've enjoyed this evening,' Jo said, and knew she spoke the truth. Up till her parting with the child. 'She's . . . she's a dear little thing.'

'Yes, poor mite.' Chrissie shook her grey head. 'To lose both parents the way she did and then . . .' She stopped and took a sip of her tea. 'There, I do go on. And Jake so hates gossiping. Sam's taken such a shine to you.' She began on another tack. 'I was quite thunderstruck when she came back from the beach all smiles, talking about her new friend Jo. To tell you the truth I thought at first she meant a little boy of her own age.'

Jo smiled.

'Well, I was pleased as punch. Usually she's so cold and shy of strangers and I worry so, as the poor little mite needs more than just Jake and me for company.' The older woman stopped to refill Jo's cup and her own.

'Of course, Jake can't be too careful,' she continued. He's had the devil of a job this past year keeping the media at bay. And when he returned home and I told him that the 'Jo' that Sam was always talking about was, as Sam described you, a pretty lady, he was quite disturbed. Until he ensured that you weren't a newspaper reporter, that is. We've been here seven months and we were just beginning to relax a little.' She shook her head. 'It was such a sad business. Jake was nearly driven mad.'

'It did cross my mind that he might be just slightly deranged when he approached me on the beach.' Jo tried to smile. 'I'm afraid he took me quite by surprise, and he was so . . . so angry.'

'I can believe it,' Chrissie laughed. 'Jake can be formidable when it comes to his privacy—and quite justifiably. The tragedy was bad enough in itself without the continuous questions and snapping of camera flashes every time he put his head out of the door.'

'What happened?' Jo enquired. 'Was it to do with Sam's parents?'

'You never heard? It was all over the newspapers and television at the time.' Chrissie remarked.

'No. No, I can't say I did.' Jo fixed her eyes on her teacup. 'I haven't—well, I haven't been well this past year, so I've lost touch with daily news and . . . and things like that.'

'Oh,' Chrissie paused, as though trying to decide whether or not to discuss the subject with Jo, 'I guess it won't hurt to fill you in. It's common knowledge, more's the pity. Jake's brother, that was Sam's father, was a television news reporter, went to all these way-out places reporting on political upheavals and revolutions or disasters and suchlike. Just over a year ago they—his wife was with him—were killed in an uprising in one of the Central American states.'

'Oh, dear, that's terrible,' Jo said quietly, and Chrissie nodded.

'Sam was with them, too, and by some miracle she was saved. Jake flew over to collect her and brought her back. It was weeks before she would even talk to anyone, poor little thing, but Jake persevered with her. He's been just wonderful and loves her as if she was his own.' Chrissie blinked back a few tears.

Somehow, on her one meeting with Jake Marshall Jo was finding it rather difficult to accredit him with the virtues Chrissie was describing. And as for Sam . . .

'Well, enough of that. What about you, Jo?' Chrissie bit into a homemade fruit square.

'Oh, nothing. There's really not . . . nothing much to tell.' Jo felt her face flush and her hand went involuntarily to pat her hair nervously in place.

'I couldn't help noticing the scar on your face.' Chrissie's own face mirrored her sympathy. 'Was it a car accident?'

Freezing in her seat, Jo fought down the inevitable urge to cry out that she didn't want to discuss it, didn't want to so much as think about it. Her eyes darted to the door and she almost stood up to rush out to her car and away. But the older woman was sitting quietly attentive and her calmness was all at once a soothing balm. Until now only Maggie had possessed that quality and Jo realised her tensed muscles had relaxed slightly.

She set her cup down a little shakily on the saucer. 'Yes,' she heard herself reply. 'Yes, it was a car accident.'

Chrissie shook her head. 'It must have been traumatic for you—but you know I wouldn't have even seen the scar if Sam hadn't told me about it. Your hair hides it quite well. I suppose you'll be having some surgery done on it before long.'

Jo's fingers made their well-known voyage of the ragged furrow and she frowned, trying to keep the million painful associations at bay. 'I don't know. I . . . Nothing's been decided yet.'

'I see. I suppose your family . . .' Chrissie pulled herself up quickly. 'There I go again, prying! Please, forgive me, Jo. I'm an interfering old busybody and my only excuse is that I love people and I'm just simply interested.'

'That's all right,' Jo reassured her. 'I'm afraid I'm a bit rusty when it comes to talking. Since . . . since the accident I've been,' Jo swallowed convulsively, 'I've had difficulty getting my life back into perspective and it seems strange to talk about it,' she finished slowly. 'The only person I've ever discussed it with is Maggie, my stepsister. My stepfather, that's Maggie's father, and Maggie's own family are the only family I have.' She swallowed again. 'My . . . my husband was killed in the accident,' she got out.

There, she'd said it. Now to tell Chrissie about Jamie, tell her that her son was killed as well. Her breath refused to flow. Say it now, something inside her urged. Say it out loud.

No! Don't think! Don't think! Her reflexes screamed at her again and she clutched her hands together until she became aware of the hardness of her wedding ring biting into the flesh on her fingers.

'My dear, how terrible for you,' Chrissie was saying softly. 'How long ago was this?'

'About . . . nearly eighteen months ago,' Jo replied woodenly.

Chrissie saw the whiteness of Jo's face and reached across to pat her arm. 'I'm so sorry. I hope I haven't upset you, bringing it all up. Perhaps you'd like another cup of tea. It wouldn't take long to boil the kettle again.'

'No, thanks. I really should be going,' Jo pushed herself to her feet. 'It's late, and I think the rain seems to have eased off a little.'

'Yes, I do believe it has.' Chrissie stood up. 'I've got an old umbrella here for you to use to get to the car.' She handed the umbrella to Jo. 'And thanks so much for coming, I've enjoyed it. And now that you know where we are you must come again.'

'Thank you, too, for the lovely meal.' Jo slipped her jacket on.

'Oh, I love cooking.' Chrissie smiled. 'And, Jo—thanks for coming, for Sam's sake, as well. You've really brought the poor little thing out of herself. Anyway, now you can understand why Jake was so worried about your motives at first.'

A wave of guilt washed over Jo when she recalled her first reaction to seeing the child on the beach. She had thought nothing of the little girl, but only of herself and her own pain, not knowing that Sam had suffered, was probably still suffering her own agonies.

The purr of a car engine rose above the patter of the light rain and as Jo and Chrissie peered into the dripping darkness twin beams of light cut across the foliage, briefly illuminating Jo's Mini before the car stopped and the engine and lights died.

'Heaven's that's Jake! He's early.'

Chrissie's words filled Jo with horror and the same almost hysterical urge to escape rose to choke her. But she couldn't move, not without pushing past Chrissie and rushing down the steps into the night. She had to stand behind the other woman, the umbrella clutched in her hand, and watch the dark figure get out of the car, flip up the collar of his coat, and dash across to the verandah in a few long, sure strides.

To Jo the next few minutes were a jumble of incoherent images, as though she was viewing stills of a movie, one after the other in quick succession. Jake Marshall, dwarfing their small section of the verandah as he opened his thigh-length coat and shook some of the raindrops from it. The impression of strength in his broad shoulders moulded in the light-coloured sweater he wore. The long length of his legs in dark tailored slacks.

His eyes, their colour indistinguishable in the semi-darkness, went straight to her as he made the top of the steps, and she wondered at his thoughts as she let her own gaze fall nervously from his.

'This is a surprise, Jake,' smiled Chrissie. 'I thought you might have decided to stay in town instead of driving back in the rain.'

'It wasn't raining when I set out,' he said in the same deep voice that Jo remembered from the beach. 'But the last half hour I had to just about crawl along.' His eyes found Jo's again. 'Miss Brent.'

Chrissie frowned and turned to Jo.

'It's ... It's Harrison. Joelle Harrison,' she said quickly, knowing her hand shook where it clutched the umbrella.

He gave a slight inclination of his head, but his eyes never left hers, burning into her until her legs began to feel weak and she suspected he could read her thoughts, see into her very soul.

'I must be going,' Jo said quickly, trying to slide the umbrella up, but it refused to move.

A strong hand closed over hers and took the umbrella from her and slid it up with seeming ease. 'I'll see you to your car,' he said, and held the umbrella ready for her so that she had to step under it.

The arm of his coat brushed hers, sending tingling shivers through her, and her hand trembled as she reached for the door handle of the Mini. Some time later she had to agree with him that her car was not going to start.

'Perhaps there's some condensation in the distributor cap,' she suggested, looking up at him as he stood beside the car with the rain dripping in cascades off the umbrella. 'I'll ... I'll try wiping it out.'

'I think it might be better if I drive you home, and I'll have a look at your car tomorrow in the daylight,' he said firmly.

'Oh, no. I ... I couldn't put you out.'

His hand closed around her arm and before she could

say another word she was out of the car and he was pocketing her ignition keys. He left her for a moment after he had settled her in the passenger seat of his car to cross back to the verandah to speak to Chrissie. When he settled behind the wheel of the plushly detailed BMW the rain had grown heavier, beating down on the car so that even the glowing headlights scarcely penetrated the wall of water.

Jo clutched her hands together in her lap, wishing she wasn't so aware of every smooth movement Jake Marshall made. With a minimum of manipulation he had turned the car back along the driveway and was driving slowly around the bay to the cottage. She closed her eyes tightly, using all her resources to blot out that other car trip she had made in the darkness of night, in the rain, and its earth-shattering aftermath. At last they were turning down the driveway and he pulled to a halt as close to her back door as possible.

The old umbrella barely coped with the water that fell upon it, and Jo had to almost shout to tell him that her house key was on the same keyring as the Mini's ignition keys he had put in his pocket.

The back door opened into the laundry, and when Jo flicked on the light the small utility room seemed even more confined than usual with Jake Marshall's large frame standing dripping as he took off his coat and folded it over the washing tubs. The umbrella also went into the laundry tubs, while Jo stood open-mouthed. Surely he didn't expect to stay? After their last meeting they could have nothing whatsoever to talk about.

He took one last look out of the door before closing it firmly and turning to face her. 'At the moment it's hard to believe the weather forecasters who assure us that all this will clear tomorrow,' he said evenly, wiping a hand over his hair. Moist droplets ran on to his thick cream sweater and he grimaced.

Unconsciously Jo reached for a clean towel lying folded on the washing machine and silently passed it to him, realising her own jacket was thoroughly soaked on one side. As he used the towel on his hair she took off the jacket and looked ruefully at her dress, the skirt of which was even wetter.

'You'd better go and change out of that,' his voice came from beneath the towel, muffled as he rubbed vigorously at the thick darkness of his hair.

'I . . . It will be all right,' she managed to get out.

'You'll be more comfortable,' he said, appearing from beneath the folds of the towel. 'I want to talk to you. About Sam,' he added, his face serious.

'What about her?' Jo asked quietly, not making any move to do as he bid.

He frowned then, lowering the towel, and Jo surprised herself by having to force down a smile at the way his hair stood every which way and it crossed her mind that he looked almost human. He must have read some of her thoughts in her eyes, for his frown deepened and he raised his head slightly, his eyes narrowing. 'Look, Miss Brent——' he shrugged irritably—'Mrs Harrison. I think we should both try to forget our last meeting. I do genuinely want to talk to you about my niece, so you have my word that you've nothing to fear from me. I'm not in the habit of coming on as strongly as I did on the beach, believe me, and I think an apology on my part is in order. I was so blazingly angry with what I mistakenly thought you were up to.'

Jo watched him carefully, and reluctantly nodded her head. 'All right. You can come through and I'll go upstairs and change.' She switched on the lights as she hurried towards the stairs, realising she was trembling all over from the cold. At least, she assured herself it was the cold.

As quickly as possible she shed her wet dress and

underclothes and pulled on a pair of dark blue corduroy slacks and a thick pale blue jumper, feeling their
dry warmth thawing the numbness as she ran a brush
through her shoulder-length blonde hair. The damp
air made it even more wavy and she noticed with relief
that its curl totally concealed the scar.

'I took the liberty of boiling the kettle,' Jake
Marshall said when she somewhat reluctantly joined
him and he passed her a steaming cup of coffee. 'Black
or white?'

'Black, thanks,' she replied, and he nodded, adding
two spoonfuls of sugar to his own black coffee. 'Shall
we sit here?' he indicated the stools at the breakfast
bar. 'Or would you prefer the living-room?'

'This will do,' Jo replied, sitting on the stool nearest
her, thankful that the second stool was on the other
side of the breakfast bar and not beside hers. At least
she could keep him at a safe distance.

Sipping her coffee, her eyes downcast, she knew his
eyes were on her and she felt herself tense to breaking
point as she waited for him to speak. When at last he
did, the sound of his voice made her jump, her eyes
going involuntarily to his face.

'I'd like to thank you for——' he paused, 'the attention you've been giving my niece. She seems quite
taken with you. You have the same colouring as her
mother,' he added flatly, his eyes going over her face,
and she clutched the tabletop to restrain her hand from
defensively covering her cheek, 'a fact which also poses
a problem.'

Jo watched him steadily, wondering what problem
he was talking about. The dull ache inside her intensified. Couldn't he understand the problem Sam
created for her? Didn't he realise the painful associations the little body catapulted into her consciousness?

'How long do you intend remaining here?' he asked
somewhat abruptly. 'I realise you don't own this

place—the Chamberlains do—so you must be renting or leasing from them, and I'd like to know how long you intend staying.'

Some long-dormant emotion was stirring within her and her frayed senses sought to define it. Irritation, almost anger. Her lips tightened at the arrogance of him as he sat opposite her demanding an answer to a question he had no prerogative to ask, as though any interrogation was his right.

'I haven't decided on any fixed time,' she said at last. 'I'm on . . . on holiday. This house belongs to my sister and brother-in-law, so fortunately I can come and go when and as I please.' With no small effort she managed to keep her eyes levelly on his.

'I see.' He was frowning, running one strong tanned long-fingered hand over his jaw.

'What do you see, Mr Marshall?' Jo heard herself ask equably, and with a shock she realised some of her old assurance and self-confidence from that old life had found its way into her voice.

His eyes flickered, as though impossibly he was momentarily disconcerted at her change of tone before his eyelids fell to shadow his expression and he watched her through narrowed eyes.

'I'm not meaning to pry into your affairs, believe me. My one aim in this case is to protect my niece.'

'From me?' Jo asked incredulously.

'From any more,' he paused, 'traumas.'

'Chrissie told me that Sam lost both her parents very tragically,' Jo said softly, 'and I'm sorry. But how could I—well——?'

Jake Marshall stood up and paced across the small kitchenette, pausing to stand with his back to her, his hand rubbing the tensed muscles in the back of his neck. His cream sweater pulled across the breadth of his solid shoulders and Jo's eyes rested on him, catching the emanative strength of his large frame.

He was all of six feet tall, his shoulders broad, his arms bulgingly muscular, and his brown slacks moulded the narrowness of his hips and the long firm hardness of his legs. She found herself involuntarily remembering the feel of that rock-hard body pressing against her as he had held her on the beach, and her heartbeats accelerated, falling over themselves in their sudden impetus.

Without warning he turned back to face her and she flushed as their eyes met and held. When his gaze centred on her lips she knew the intensification of a kaleidoscope of tingling sensations of awareness that flowed across the short distance between them.

Jo swallowed convulsively and the hand holding her coffee cup trembled slightly before she rattled the cup into the saucer.

'How could you create a problem?' Jake repeated as he crossed to her and sat down again on the stool. 'That's the trouble. I don't quite know. In some ways you're an unknown quantity, Miss Brent.'

'Harrison,' Jo corrected automatically through tensed lips.

He raised one dark eyebrow and reached across the breakfast bar to take hold of her left hand, his fingers fastening firmly about her wrist, his eyes regarding the thin gold wedding band.

'I've done some checking up today as well,' he said reflectively. 'On you. So I suppose you could say that I know quite a lot about you, Joelle Brent Harrison.'

CHAPTER FOUR

Jo could only stare at him, her mind numb. She knew she should make some attempt to deny any knowledge of what he was talking about, protect herself in some way, tell him that he was mistaken, that his time had been wasted. But no words came, although she must have shaken her head, for he lifted one eyebrow again.

'No? I think "yes",' he said softly. 'Even if they didn't know your name nine out of ten people in the street would recognize your face. It was, after all, an extensive advertising campaign. And any theatregoer would know Joelle Brent. You were a very well-known actress.'

Realising he still had hold of her hand, Jo tried to pull away from him. 'Please let me go!'

His fingers tightened. 'Well, Joelle Brent Harrison, weren't you a very well-known actress?'

' "Were" is the operative word, Mr Marshall,' Jo replied flatly. 'Past tense. Although I can't see that it's any of your business.'

'Maybe not,' he shrugged. 'But Sam is my business. And she's been a very disturbed little girl. She's just started to come out of it, and I've no intention of allowing anything or anyone to drag her backwards. I'm afraid that has to include you.'

'And I have to repeat, how could I do that?' Jo asked tersely. 'In what way could I harm Sam?'

He paused for a moment before replying. 'By devoting time to her, attention if you like, and then leaving just as suddenly as you arrived.'

'Mr Marshall, I did not seek your niece out,' Jo began.

'I know that,' he frowned. 'Unfortunately you just happened to be there at the time when Sam began to venture farther than the door of the house. Each time we moved we spent literally weeks regaining her confidence of the new environment.' He sighed. 'Anyway, she talks about you constantly. I suspect she sees in you an image of the mother she lost.'

Jo saw a momentary impression of pain on the lines of his face before the set mask fell in place. The familiar ache began to gnaw at her again and she shook her head, standing up abruptly and pulling her hand from his hold. Wrapping her arms about her body protectively, she turned away.

'Look, I didn't intend to upset you.' Jake strode around the breakfast bar towards her.

Jo swung around to face him with her hand held out to ward him off, backing away as he strode forward. He stopped just as suddenly as he had moved and ran his hand through his still damp hair.

'Perhaps I'm making more out of this thing with Sam, imagining bogey men who don't exist, but surely you can see I can't afford not to go into all aspects of the situation.'

All aspects. Jo could almost laugh. In fact a laugh of sorts did escape her, and as she stood off from herself she suspected she was bordering on hysteria. And it was all because of Jake Marshall. If he knew so much about her then why couldn't he realise the agony he was inflicting on her? Didn't he know that every child who crossed her path, even her own stepsister's two little girls, was a heartrending reminder of the only piece of innocence, or reality, in the star-spangle-façaded empty life she had led?

A grey mist seemed to shroud them. Someone somewhere nearby was making a terrific noise, a high-pitched cry like an animal in pain, and she tried to shut her ears to it. Then she felt hard bands of steel grasp her shoulders and her head lolled about as she was vigorously shaken and her hair fell back from her face. But still the noise continued until a loud crack echoed about the room and a physical pain spread over her cheek.

She put one hand to the unmarked side of her face and stared up at Jake through a curtain of tears. All sound had disappeared, leaving a thick heavy silence save for the distant roar of the waves on the beach. Somewhere Jo's mind also registered irrelevantly that it had stopped raining.

Blinking rapidly, she brought his face into sharper focus as she realised the actuality of the situation. He had slapped her face because she had lost control. Dignity surfaced from the churning sea of her emotions. How dared he? Before there had always been a sedative, a soft soothing. Not a harsh assault that sent waves of stinging pain from the numbness of her bruised face.

'I'm sorry I had to do that,' he said flatly. 'I couldn't seem to get you out of it any other way.'

'How dare you . . . How dare you do . . . do that to me!' Jo's words fell out of her mouth almost incoherently, mixed with gulping sobs. 'How dare you hit me!'

His jaw tightened. 'You were hysterical and you weren't responding to my gentle pleas so I had to use the last resort.'

Tears blinded her again, overflowing to course down her cheeks. She heard him catch his breath as his hands pulled her against his hard body, one strong arm going around her, the other hand holding her head against his chest. 'What brought that on?' he asked softly, and Jo could only shake her head into the warmth of his chest.

Gradually she relaxed against him, most of her tension leaving her and her sobs subsided. Her face rested on the thickness of his sweater and she grew aware of the closeness, the heady muskiness of his aftershave and the steady thump of his heart beneath her hand. This awareness brought with it another kind of tension that held Jo motionless. Somewhere deep inside a warming rising tide began to thaw the numbness, causing the blood to pound throughout her body and bringing alive all the tantalising sensations she thought had been buried within her, and she raised her head to look up at him. She was unaware of the uncertainty, the vulnerability in the bright softness of her eyes as they met and held his.

She saw a pulse beating in the line of his jaw and felt the variance in the poise of his body still touching hers. Beneath her hand his heartbeat had changed rhythm and his eyes darkened. When his lips came slowly down to claim hers she made no effort to move away, to deny him, and a small sigh opened her lips to his as his mouth gently caressed hers.

His arms slid further about her, pulling her closer to the solid length of him as his kiss hardened, taking her response, and demanding a surrender.

Jo's hands had crept around him, slid beneath the rollneck collar of his sweater to caress the hardness of his neck, to move upwards to luxuriate in the damp thickness of his dark hair. His lips teased her earlobe, moved down the softness of her throat, and she felt her own trembling being echoed in his own body.

He raised his head to look down at her, his eyes settling on each feature, stopping on the fullness of her slips, and as he bent his head to claim them once more she heard him murmur her name in a voice thick with heightened desire.

'My God! You're so beautiful,' he said almost to himself, his kisses driving her along with him, surging towards the point of no return.

And Jo knew and recognised how little resistance

she seemed to have to this man and a minute gnawing of fear began to eat at her, grew until it gained the upper hand and she pushed both hands against his chest putting a little space between them.

'Jo?' His voice was deeply husky and he made to pull her back into his arms.

'No. Please,' Jo began, her hands still on his chest fending him off.

For incalculable seconds he held her fast and then his hands fell away and the gap between them widened, became a yawning chasm and, suddenly cold, Jo began to shiver, yearned for the warmth of his nearness.

'I think perhaps I should be going,' he said flatly, 'while there's some easing off of the rain.' He crossed to the kitchenette and Jo took a few tentative steps after him, her hand out, wanting desperately to call him back, but her head overruled her heart's directions and her hand fell to her side.

In the utility room Jake shrugged on his coat and turned back towards her as he straightened his collar, his eyes dark and unfathomable.

'Thank you . . .' Jo paused, her throat tight.

He raised one eyebrow sardonically. 'It was my pleasure,' he remarked suggestively, and Jo felt herself flush.

'For . . . for driving me home,' she added quickly, her hands clasping agitatedly together.

One corner of his mouth rose in a cynical smile and he inclined his head almost imperceptibly. 'I repeat— my pleasure. Goodnight, Miss Brent.'

Jo stood by the door as his car purred easily up to the road and the red dots of his tail-lights disappeared into the chilly blackness.

Slowly she locked the back door and switched off each light as she moved back into the kitchen. Robotlike she collected their coffee cups and rinsed them out, leaving them to drain on the sink. When she found herself upstairs in the bedroom she stood blinking at her reflection in the dressing table mirror and her fingers slowly went to her slightly swollen mouth as she recalled the sensations evoked by the demanding pressure of Jake's lips on hers. Her eyes looked back at her, large and dark in her pale face, their expression softly bewildered.

Just remembering Jake's lips on hers, his hard body pressed against hers, sent her senses spinning erratically out of control, any thought of resisting him banished as though it didn't exist. And perhaps it didn't. Her body seemed to take over, to dominate her mind.

She sank down on the bed. If he'd wanted to stay tonight she would barely have put up even a token resistance. My God, she thought, what could be happening to her? She had never been like that before. Even when she was a student at the Academy she had always kept herself apart from any sexual involvements, had never been tempted to enter into any closer relationships with the young men she knew. She had always been too involved with her acting, and even with Mike . . . Yes, even with Mike she had never had to make any great effort not to want a physical relationship until they were married. They had argued about it a number of times and she had always remained firm.

And now here she was responding to a man she had barely met with an abandonment of which she scarcely knew she was capable. It was unbelievable. And terrifying.

She began to tremble. Surely the accident hadn't robbed her of the ability to hold firm in her basic belief of what was right and what was wrong? It couldn't have. She knew in herself right at this moment what her moral standards were. But Jake Marshall only had to look at her with those deep dark blue eyes of his and she seemed to lose all . . .

How she wished Maggie was here to talk to. Maggie would be calm and sensible, tell her that it was a natural physical reaction she would feel towards any attractive man after all this time. She reached out for the phone and began to dial, only to replace the receiver half way through Maggie's number. She couldn't disturb Maggie this late at night. She would think something was wrong and only worry about her.

But something *was* wrong. That was the whole point, and it all seemed to be snowballing out of her control. She was beginning to feel again, to experience, to respond, and she had no desire to do that. She wanted nothing more of those heady sensations. Without feeling meant without pain. No agony of loss. No empty yearning . . .

She wrapped her arms about herself again in that same gesture of self-protection, her stomach turning over with nervous despair. She couldn't afford to allow herself to feel again. She hadn't the strength to face any of the traumas she knew from past experience went with the kind of relationship that Jake Marshall's kisses preluded.

Standing up, she held herself stiffly and forced her thoughts to a resolution. She would just have to sever all ties with the Marshalls, that was all it amounted to. She had to protect herself, guard the fragile shield, the tentative shell she had begun to grow around the shattered remnants of the person she had been.

Sam's plain little face swam before her and her teeth bit into her lip. No matter what decision Jo made the child would be hurt. Better to make the break now at this early stage than allow the situation to develop any further.

The pain tugged at Jo's heartstrings once again. The poor little scrap had endured so much in her short life. How could fate be so unkind? What cruel coincidence had manoeuvred Jo to this particular spot just when the child was needing so badly a substitute for the mother she had lost so tragically? And why did it have to be her? Sam was an innocent child. She couldn't know the agony of memories her thin little arms wrapped about Jo's neck could evoke, the big blue eyes looking up with complete unquestioning trust.

Stifling a sob, Jo lay back on the bed. Yes, the tie must be cut. As soon as Jake Marshall returned her car the next morning she would leave, go back to Maggie for a few days until she found somewhere else, another bolthole in which to lick her wounds.

Another escape, said a small voice inside her, and she sat up stiffly. What if she did need an escape? Was that too much to need after all that had happened? There had to be a limit to the pain a person could endure before they broke, gave in to the agony. And Jo knew she had reached and gone beyond that point a long time ago. Now she had no desire to go back, to take one heavy emotion-charged footstep towards a new beginning. There was nothing of her world remaining to go back to.

With astounding suddenness Jake Marshall's strong face appeared on the screen of her memory, erasing all others, and the same quickening of her senses sent a series of tremors through the wasteland of what she had considered dead and forgotten experiences. The picture before her eyes was so clear and well defined, each detail sketched in with a vivid recall, that had she reached out her hand she felt she would encounter his hard body standing there before her.

Blue eyes so dark they appeared almost black, with dark lashes and fine dark eyebrows. The neatness of his hair styled relatively short in the front but lying neatly down to his collar at the back. When her re-collection centred on his lips she began to tremble again, remembering their cool firmness moving on her own lips, hardening, demanding. And her response . . .

Leaning forward, Jo covered her face with her hands, trying to erase that graphic image, free herself of the web of desire he could weave about her vulnerable emotions.

Don't think! Don't think! she screamed at herself. It was simply a physical thing. He was just another attractive male. She had met his kind before. She had moved in a world of attractive men, and she'd coped with them all, so she could cope with Jake Marshall. At any rate after tomorrow she wouldn't need to cope with him, she told herself, for after tomorrow she would be gone and Jake Marshall could slip unceremoniously into the foggy faraway of her precluded past.

It was a long time before she finally drifted off to sleep and when she awoke heavy-eyed the sun had found its way through the light blanket of cloud and it was well into the morning. A quick shower did much to alleviate the dull aching behind her eyes, and she sighed tiredly as she walked slowly downstairs to brew herself a cup of tea.

Sitting at the breakfast bar, her hands wrapped around the hot cup, she could almost convince herself that to move on to another beach shack or mountain hideaway was just what she needed. And from that thought her mind flowed through an almost natural progression of impressions to Jake Marshall.

Of course she would have to face him again when he returned the car. She glanced at the clock on the wall, wondering what time he would come, how long she had to prepare herself. Most probably he would turn up any time now. She began to consciously steel herself, sitting up straighter, holding her head up, hoping she would appear calm and composed. And aloof.

He had only kissed her, when all was said and done, and in this day and age of free thought a few kisses meant next to nothing. In the tinsel fantasy of the world she had lived in before the accident a kiss was an accepted greeting. But not the type of kiss that she had exchanged last night with Jake Marshall, she told herself harshly. No one had ever kissed her the way Jake Marshall had assaulted her defences. Not even Mike.

Her stiffened backbone slumped weakly. Not even Mike, she repeated to herself, and a small ripple of guilt washed over her. She knew the unrest in her marriage was a lot of her own making and, their disagreement over Jamie apart, she would most probably still have left her husband.

She drew a quivering breath as the dreaded memories began to flood over her. Don't think! Don't think!

Resolutely she stood up and ran the hot water to wash her breakfast dishes and the coffee cups from the night before, keeping her mind totally on the job in hand. Then she walked through to the laundry to see to the drying of her wet clothes. A few hours in the weak sunlight would take away the dampness.

Opening the back door, she stood clutching the clothes to her. There was her Mini already parked in its usual place. Jake must have returned the car while she slept. The keys were on the driver's seat, sitting on a familiar piece of thick notepaper that had been folded once.

'Car shouldn't give you any trouble now.' And it was signed simply with his initials. A spurt of anger gripped her. Just the flourish of those two letters was a stark illustration of his assurance, his arrogance. She crushed the sheet of paper in her hand. She should be grateful that she hadn't had to face him. Now she could leave without having any further contact with him—or the child. A slow chill gripped her heart and she moved resolutely back to the house, firmly telling herself that this coldness of regret was totally for Sam and had nothing whatsoever to do with the child's overbearing uncle.

Two hours later Jo had cleaned the house and packed her two suitcases with her clothes and belongings. All that was left to collect together were the few perishable foodstuffs that couldn't be left behind. There was at last no reason for her to remain, but strangely now she had a reluctance to leave. The place was, after all, ideal. It had been—past tense. Everything was now in the past tense. And if it hadn't been for the Marshalls she could have . . .

A loud banging on the back door nearly frightened her out of her wits. She stood immobile until Sam's almost hysterical voice calling her name over and over suddenly penetrated her startled consciousness. Jo was at the door in a couple of strides, and as she wrenched it open Sam's distraught figure flew into her arms, huge gulping sobs racking the thin little body.

It was some time before the child was coherent enough for Jo to piece some of Sam's words together. She sat the little girl on the bench top beside the sink and gently sponged her face.

'Calm down now, Sam, and tell me exactly what happened to Chrissie.' Jo feigned an outward calmness.

'She . . . she fell down,' Sam got out, 'down the steps at the front, and she . . . she can't get up again.' Fresh sobs shook her body. 'You must come, Jo! Chrissie said to run over and get you and I did. I ran along the road as fast as I could. Will you come, Jo?'

'Of course.' Jo lifted Sam down and hurried out to the Mini, a hundred horrific thoughts racing around inside her imagination.

The car started immediately and Jo had them back to the Marshall house in no time. Sam ran around the side of the house with Jo close behind, dreading what she was about to find.

'Her eyes are closed.' Sam pulled to a sudden halt, her face as white as a sheet. 'Oh, Jo, is she dead?' The small hand on Jo's arm tightened in fear.

Jo bent down and lifted the older woman's hand to feel her pulse, but at her touch Chrissie's eyes fluttered open.

'Thank God!' she said weakly. 'I so hoped you'd be home, Jo.'

'Oh, Chrissie, you're not dead!' Sam threw herself on to the ground beside the woman, one hand gently patting Chrissie's arm.

'No, of course I'm not, love.' Chrissie's pain-filled eyes rested on the child and she took hold of Sam's hand as she turned back to Jo. 'I think I've broken my leg. I can't seem to move myself.'

'I'll . . . I'll call the doctor.' Jo knelt back, trying not to let either Chrissie or Sam see the shock she felt at the sight of the older woman's leg lying at such an unnatural angle. 'Is his number handy?'

Chrissie nodded weakly. 'In the book by the telephone. Dr Hodges.'

Jo stood up. 'You stay and talk to Chrissie, Sam, while I call the doctor.' She disappeared inside, her fingers fumbling over the pages of the alphabetical index, as she searched frantically for the doctor's number.

'They're on their way,' she said thankfully as she rejoined Chrissie and Sam, tucking the rug she'd found in the living-room over Chrissie's prostrate form.

In twenty minutes the doctor had arrived, followed by the ambulance, and Chrissie was wheeled inside and borne away to have her leg X-rayed and plastered. Jo and Sam followed the ambulance in the Mini and stayed with Chrissie for as long as possible.

As the orderly went to wheel her away Chrissie clutched urgently at Jo's hand. 'Sam. You will . . . you will look after her until her uncle gets home?' she asked agitatedly. 'Won't you, Jo?'

'Of course. Now don't you worry about Sam,' Jo tried to set the older woman's mind at rest.

'Oh, thank you, Jo. For everything.' Tears glistened in Chrissie's eyes. 'I just dread to think what would have happened if you hadn't been nearby.' She swallowed a sob. 'Jake shouldn't be late. He said he hoped to be back by nine o'clock.'

Jo squeezed Chrissie's hand before standing back to allow her to be wheeled away.

'Will Chrissie be all right tomorrow?' Sam's eyes fixed on Jo as hand in hand they walked out of the Casualty Ward to the car park.

'Well, it will take some time for her leg to heal,' Jo said carefully. 'The doctor will have to bandage her leg up so that the broken bone will mend properly.'

'How long will she be away?' Sam asked tearfully.

'I don't know. That depends on where exactly her leg is broken and how easy it is to fix it.' Jo unlocked the car door and sat Sam inside, buckling up the safety belt.

'Jo?'

'Yes?' Jo turned in her seat to face the child.

'When we get back will you stay with me till Uncle Jake comes home?' Sam asked.

A lump rose in Jo's throat, threatening to choke her, and she put her arms comfortingly about the child. 'Of course I will. I promised Chrissie I'd look after you, so we'll go back and have some dinner and we can telephone the hospital to see how Chrissie is when your . . . when your uncle comes homes.'

'Oh, Jo! I really didn't want to stay in the house by myself,' Sam breathed thankfully into Jo's shoulder. 'I'm so very glad you'll be with me. I get . . . I get scared in the dark by myself.'

By eight o'clock the drama-fraught day had taken its

toll and Sam's eyelids began to droop. She went a little reluctantly to bed until Jo promised to sit with her, and she was fast asleep before Jo had finished reading the story she chose.

With the little girl asleep Jo found herself a trifle unsure of how to fill in the time until Jake Marshall returned. She made herself a cup of tea and sat in the kitchen savouring its warmth, trying not to think about having to face him again. Her fingers trembled and she wrapped them tightly about her teacup, wishing her heartbeats didn't race, stirring her nervous system to echo their racing tattoo.

So much for her not having to see him again, she thought wryly. And she refused to think about how Chrissie's stay in hospital would affect Jake Marshall and his niece. He would have to hire another house-keeper until Chrissie was well enough to take up her old position.

By the time Jo had rinsed and dried her cup and tidied it away Jake still hadn't arrived home. Feeling an unwarranted guilt, as though she was trespassing, Jo explored the layout of the house.

It was larger than she had thought it was, looking at it from the outside when she came to dinner the night before, and besides Sam's room there appeared to be three other bedrooms and two bathrooms. She hastily withdrew from the open doorway of what was obviously a masculine room, her mind recording the sweater thrown over the bed and the austere dressing table.

The only room left to investigate opened off the living-room and she tried the doorknob, half expecting it, for some reason, to be locked, but it swung inwards at her touch and she felt for the light switch. It was a comfortable room, quite large, and she was surprised at the number of books that lined the shelves on each wall. To one side was a sturdy desk on which sat a typewriter, neatly covered by its dust cover, and behind the desk was an adjustable typist's chair looking very workmanlike and functional compared to the large leather-covered chair near the curtained window.

Jo walked across the thick-pile carpet to run her hand over the soft deep brown leather. In a neat pile on the small coffee table beside the chair were three or four books, all marked with thick pieces of white paper on which a familiar bold hand had written short references. She carefully lifted the top one and glanced at the spine, raising her eyebrows at the title, a textbook of forensic medicine. The other three books were also relating to criminal law and investigatory techniques.

Replacing the books, Jo stepped across to the nearest bookshelf and her eyes skimmed the titles. Before the accident she had been an inveterate reader, regretting that she didn't have more time to spend on the pastime. If this room was anything to go by Jake Marshall had a very catholic taste in reading matter himself.

A green-covered book caught her attention and she lifted it out, her lips twisting in a smile. It was a favourite author of hers and she couldn't imagine how an historical romance had found its way into Jake Marshall's library. Slowly she opened the cover and read the name written with an unformed almost childish hand on the title page: Denise Willis.

Sitting down in the leather chair, Jo felt its softness fold around her and with the book open on her lap she began to read, soon lost in the rediscovery of a story she knew she had enjoyed. At some stage, not long after the heroine had been kidnapped and borne across the Channel to France, Jo must have dozed off, and she barely stirred when the book slipped to the floor as she settled herself more comfortably in the depths of the chair.

At any rate, she failed to hear the slam of a car door much later or the footsteps striding firmly across the verandah, to the back door, pausing momentarily before the door swung open, to continue on into the house.

Something touched her cheek, gently and warmly, pleasantly dreamlike, and she smiled faintly as she floated towards wakefulness. Her head was supported on her arm and she stretched stiffly while her other hand went to her cheek to investigate that fleeting caress. She must have been dreaming, a very nice all-encompassing dream, and she sighed softly as her eyelids fluttered open.

Her gaze met and held the deep dark blue of Jake Marshall's as he leant over her chair, one hand on the arm on either side of her, imprisoning her, and she caught her breath and held it trapped.

How long they looked at each other Jo couldn't have told, for the moment was so emotion-filled that it was impossible for her to even think coherently, and it was Jake who broke the stillness of their immobility.

Slowly he reached down to retrieve the book she had been reading glancing at the cover before setting it on the table with the others.

'I was reading ... I must have fallen asleep,' Jo stammered, wishing he would move away so that she could put at least the width of the room between them, escape from his magnetic nearness. 'What time is it?'

'The wrong side of midnight,' he said evenly.

'Oh.' Jo was surprised. 'You're late,' she said softly, her words echoing her thoughts before she could stop them.

One dark eyebrow rose. 'And you sound like a wife,' he remarked just as quietly.

Jo's face suffused with colour. 'I'm sorry. I ... It's just that we expected you ... that is ... Chrissie said you'd be home about nine o'clock.'

'I was held up,' he said, his eyes moving downwards to focus on her lips, and a quiver of pure desire raced through her to hold her in its grip. How she wanted him to kiss her, to feel those firm lips take possession of hers once more. Her lips parted slightly, the tip of her tongue beginning to moisten their sudden dryness when Jake moved suddenly, standing upright, putting the space she'd wanted before between them.

But now it was a cold empty chasm, and Jo gazed up at him as he stood looking down at her, his eyelids veiling the expression in his eyes, and she wished she had the nerve to stand up and walk across to close that distance again, be wrapped close against the protective warmth of him.

'Talking about Chrissie,' he said at last, and Jo blinked, trying to get her scattered thoughts together, 'perhaps you'd like to tell me just what the hell's been going on here.'

CHAPTER FIVE

SITTING down, almost lost in the depths of the arm-chair, put Jo at a decided disadvantage and she began to struggle out of her half sitting, half lying position. Jake Marshall crossed the room and held out his hand to pull her upright. She looked at that long-fingered hand, suddenly reluctant to touch him, wishing she could simply ignore his offer of assistance. But of course it would be churlish to refuse, and she hesitantly put her hand into his.

With a minimum of effort she was standing out of the chair, momentarily so close to him she imagined she could feel the warmth of his body, the pull of attraction that enticed her closer. Just as suddenly he had moved away, before the blush that washed over her had reached her cheeks, and when she shot one quick glance at him he was leaning casually back against his desk, one long leg crossed over the other, strong arms folded.

Unbidden the thought flashed into Jo's mind that he would have no trouble at all finding women to fawn over him, and she was quite certain he could be selective in his choice. There was no doubt that he was by far the most attractive man she had ever seen, and that very same seemingly unconscious magnetism he exuded was most definitely a danger. To join what must surely be a long line of hopeful females intent upon claiming Jake Marshall's attention was the very last thing Jo needed to do.

Her eyes travelled upwards over the cream corduroy slacks he wore, skimming quickly over his flat stomach to the breadth of his shoulders moulded by his matching cream corduroy jacket. The contrasting dark brown shirt was open at the neck, the collar lying back from the strong column of his throat, and as Jo's eyes finally met his her blush deepened.

He raised one straight dark eyebrow and Jo suspected he knew she had no control over her need to look at, her desire to admire the animal grace of him. Her mouth was dry and she was unable to drag her gaze from him. Her eyes still continued to absorb, to commit to memory each feature, the firm square jaw shadowed with the daily growth of his beard. His almost black hair still slightly ruffled by the wind. The deep unfathomable blue of his eyes, like the velvety shroud of a moonless night. Or the impenetrable unknown of deep dark water.

'Well?' he asked into the quietness, his voice soft, its deep resonance startling Jo's newly revitalised nerve endings to tingling awareness.

'Sam's in bed—asleep,' she began.

'I realise that,' he said evenly. 'I checked her room first when no one answered my call.'

'I'm sorry, I didn't hear you.' Jo's hands clutched restively at each other. 'I must have dozed off.' She swallowed nervously.

'Where's Chrissie?' he asked patiently.

'She had a fall, out on the front steps,' Jo replied, and he pushed himself away from the desk, his hands going to rest on his hips as he waited for her to continue.

'She's in hospital. Her . . . her leg was broken,' Jo continued. 'But I rang before Sam went to bed and they said she was resting comfortably. The doctor said it was a clean break and that there seemed to be no complications. She's just a little shocked.'

'I see,' One hand absently rubbed his square jaw and he frowned thoughtfully. 'She'll be in hospital for some time, then,' he said almost to himself.

'For a week, perhaps,' said Jo. 'She'll be in plaster for a fair while, I should imagine.'

Jake nodded slowly and turned to lean on his hands on the desk top. 'She'll most probably need to convalesce. If she comes back here she'll only overdo it, so her sister's place in town might be the solution.'

Jo watched him in profile as he continued to frown reflectively. She took one tentative step towards him, wanting to be close to him, and as the thought crossed her mind she stopped just as suddenly, horrified at herself, not wanting to try to understand the turmoil churning within her.

She must have made some involuntary sound, for he turned his head and Jo took a deep steadying breath. 'I'm afraid I'll have to be going home now,' she said quickly as the warning bells within her chimed loudly in unison. She must escape. 'I promised Chrissie I'd take care of Sam until you returned,' she finished breathlessly.

Jake straightened then. 'Yes, I'm sorry I didn't make it home earlier.'

'That's all right. I . . . well, I'll be going.' Jo turned towards the door, her body seeming stiff and not her own. 'Goodnight,' she said as he reached around from behind her to open the door.

'Good morning, actually,' he said drily, his warm breath fanning her ear so that she had to force herself not to shy away from him. 'It's two o'clock,' he told her, glancing at his watch.

'Yes.' Jo's voice sounded thick in her ears as she stepped out on to the verandah, shivering slightly as the cool sea dampness penetrated her light blouse.

'Jo?'

He said her name quietly and she stopped and turned timorously back to face him.

'Thanks for your help today, with Sam and Chrissie. I appreciate it.'

Jo nodded, a lump inexplicably closing her throat, and turned back towards the Mini. When she had reversed the car she glanced back to see him standing on the verandah still watching her.

Once again sleep somehow eluded her when she finally climbed up to bed. She had had to open her suitcase to find her nightgown, promising herself that she would be off back to Maggie's in the morning. Chrissie's accident had only delayed her departure by one day.

Plumping her pillow, she rolled on to her stomach, setting her cheek on her hand. The imprint of the ridge of the scar brought a stillness to her restless body, and she raised her head and her fingers moved over her face. She hadn't consciously thought about her disfigurement all day, nor had her fingers moved to cover it. Even at the hospital she had been too worried about Chrissie and Sam.

The thought guiltily crossed her mind that today she had been concentrating on someone else, on the feelings of two other people and not on her own. Today, for the first time since the accident, she hadn't been wrapped tightly in the cocoon of self-inquisition, of self-awareness, of self-pity, that had become part of her, had grown about her like a second skin.

But why shouldn't she feel pity for herself, she argued in her defense. And why did she suddenly feel the need to defend herself. It had all been so easy before she came down here to the beach. Now, for some reason, she was beginning to feel trapped, as though she had stumbled into a spider's web and could not shake off its cloying silky threads. And in the centre of the web was Jake Marshall, who held for her an undeniable attraction. Then there was the child . . .

Jo turned agitatedly on to her back. She was being backed into an emotional corner, and the fear of it gripped her entire body because she was unsure of her ultimate reaction. In the old days she would have taken it all in her stride, coolly and confidently sidestepped the whole situation. But now ... Now she had a definite mistrust of herself and her actions. Since the accident she had often stood away from herself, horrified at the change, disbelieving the person she had become.

Apprehension washed over her again. There was no choice. She had no alternative but to flee before the web of Jake Marshall and his niece bound her too tightly for her to escape.

Her restless night took its toll and it was well into the morning again when she awoke. Slowly she repacked her nightclothes and donned a pair of well-worn slacks and a light sweater that would be comfortable for driving back to Maggie's.

And she must phone Maggie too, she mused over her morning cup of tea. It seemed ages since she had spoken to Maggie, so much had happened in so short a time. She wondered how her stepsister would take the news that she was returning. Jo sighed. Maggie would accept her decision without argument. She always did.

The subdued purr of a car coming down the driveway had Jo on her feet, her thoughts loudly suggesting it had to be Maggie, refusing to admit to herself that the refined quietness of the engine could only belong to Jake Marshall's BMW. Two doors slammed and then a small hand was knocking on the back door.

'Jo! Jo! It's Sam,' called the child. 'And Uncle Jake, too,' she added, her voice filled with excitement, leaving Jo in no doubt that this fact could only be an added bonus for Jo.

Jo's heartbeats rose and fell in quick succession and her palms were moist as her hand turned the door knob. Sam flew inside, her arms wrapping themselves about her waist.

'Hi, Jo! Why didn't you stay at our place last night? We had another room.'

Over the child's head Jo's eyes met Jake's as he walked across towards them, his face set in an expressionless mask.

'My own bed was waiting for me here,' Jo replied lamely, her hand involuntarily brushing the little girl's thin brownish hair back from her face. 'Have you seen ... How's Chrissie?'

'We're going to see her now, aren't we, Uncle Jake?' Sam turned to take hold of her uncle's hand. 'Uncle Jake rang the hospital before and the doctor said Chrissie was fine. Do you want to come to the hospital with us, too, Jo?'

'Well, I don't . . .' Jo stopped. Now was the time to tell them she was leaving. Perhaps she could say she had been called away urgently. But somehow, as she looked down into the bright eyes of the child, seeing Sam's small fingers clasped tightly in Jake's large tanned hand held her back. The words wouldn't come.

'Let me get a word in, Sam.' Jake spoke for the first time, his deep voice softly rebuking the little girl before he looked back at Jo. 'I'd like to talk to you, please, Mrs Harrison. May we come inside?'

'Of course. I'm sorry.' Jo stood back with a sinking feeling of wariness.

Sam skipped into the living room to stand at the large plate glass window overlooking the beach. Tensely, Jo followed her and sat weakly down on the edge of the lounge chair, her hands in her lap, watching Jake as he strode casually to the window to stand behind his niece.

'You have a great view,' he remarked.

'Yes. It's . . . it's very peaceful.' Jo replied stiltedly, her tension mounting.

He turned back to face her, one hand absently rubbing his jaw, his eyes not missing the suitcases standing by the doorway. Jo fixed her own gaze somewhere about his chin, not wanting to meet the deep blueness of his eyes, nor have her attention settle on his disturbing mouth.

'I'm in something of a jam,' he said, and in surprise Jo's eyes rose to meet his. 'I need your help.'

'In what way?' Jo asked. Surely he couldn't want her to have the child over here?

'Chrissie's accident presents me with a problem,' he was continuing. 'Couple that with the fact that Sam's grandmother is away in Adelaide visiting her daughter who's about to have her first child and I'm left with no one to look after Sam for me.' He paused. 'I thought of you.'

'But surely you would be at home with her,' Jo began, horrified at his suggestion. To be with the child all day . . . No! She couldn't! How could he even suggest it? She had a sinking feeling that the plain little scrap could become special to her, and she couldn't allow that. Never again would she permit anyone to come that close, cause that much pain.

She shot a look at Sam, who was tracing the floral pattern on the curtains with one small finger, and her heart contracted. Maybe the child needed her. And perhaps you need the child, said a small voice inside her, but she quickly put that thought from her mind, refusing to give it any credence.

'Sure I'll be home with Sam. But I'll be working fairly solidly for the next few weeks as I have a deadline to meet.' He ran his hand distractedly through his hair and as he raised his arm his light sweater rose above his belt, uncovering a few inches of firm tanned midriff.

Jo forced her eyes to travel back to his face and he sighed.

'As I said, it would only be for a few weeks, a month at the most, and I'd pay you well. Sam's a good child. You wouldn't have any trouble with her.'

At that moment the little girl ran across to Jo, kneeling down and resting her elbows in Jo's lap. 'Say you'll come and stay with us, Jo. We need you. And I promise to be very good. Chrissie would like you to, she said so on the phone, didn't she, Uncle Jake?'

The child turned to appeal to her uncle, who stood there, hands on hips, regarding Jo through half closed eyes.

'Oh, Sam, I don't know. I was about to go back up to town,' Jo began to explain.

The little girl's face fell. 'You mean,' her bottom lip trembled, 'you mean you don't want to come over and stay with Uncle Jake and me?' she asked with tears in her voice.

'It's not that I don't want to come over, Sam. It's just that I . . .' She paused, her eyes moving from the child's distressed face to meet the bland expression in Jake's eyes, and it crossed her mind that he had purposely brought the child along to achieve his own ends.

Jo fumed, wishing she could give vent to her rage and tell him just how low she thought he was. He was using his niece to get a baby-sitter so that he wouldn't have to be put out by any domestic upheaval. And he knew she wouldn't be able to resist the pleading in the child's eyes. Her eyes flashed like shot diamonds and she was sure there was some small measure of amused satisfaction in the half lift of the corners of Jake's mouth.

'Please come, Jo?' The little voice caught her attention again.

A hundred disquieting thoughts waged war inside her head, one of the foremost being the knowledge that she would have to share a house with this despicable, yet magnetic, man. Her heart fluttered in her throat as her senses registered anticipated awareness and more than a little alarming apprehension.

'You can have your very own room,' put in Sam earnestly.

'Maybe Sam could come over here?' She looked up at Jake and he shrugged his shoulders.

'I'd prefer to have you come over to the house,' he said evenly. 'Then I'd know you were both'—was there an emphasis on that word? '—safe,' he finished. 'Also, when I'm working I don't like to bother with fixing meals, etc., and I would appreciate having someone there to see to things like that. Somewhat selfish of me, I know, but . . .' He raised his hands and let them fall, his eyes meeting hers rather challengingly.

Glorified chief cook and bottlewasher was what it amounted to, Jo told herself. He had the most colossal nerve! At that moment he smiled at her, and while a tiny part of her tried to tell her that smile was his trump card her traitorous senses had already succumbed to the charm he was exuding. His eyes crinkled at the corners and a deep furrow appeared on either side of his mouth as his lips curved upwards.

'You won't see much of me,' he added. 'I've been held up these past few weeks what with one thing and another, so I'll be working solidly from dawn till dusk.'

'Well——' Jo began, still slightly breathless. She knew she should refuse outright. It was the safest thing to do, to cut and run. But she hovered uncertainly, wanting yet not wanting to follow the dictates of her conscious mind.

Jake turned slowly and walked back to the window, leaving her to make her decision.

Sam's small hand tapped her on the knee and after a conspiratorial look at her uncle's back she leant forward to whisper to Jo, 'Please say you will, 'cause if you don't I think Uncle Jake might ask Lexie and I just couldn't bear for *her* to stay.'

'What's that, Sam?' Jake swung back to his niece and the little girl looked guiltily at the floor.

'It's all right,' said Jo, although she wasn't exactly sure for whose benefit. 'I'll . . . I'll come.'

'You will?' Sam's eyes lit up with delight. 'Oh, Jo, that's great!' She hurled herself into Jo's arms. 'Really great,' she breathed against Jo's neck.

Over the little girl's head Jo's eyes met Jake's, and she thought wryly to herself that she could have chosen more descriptive adjectives, and none of them were complimentary to her sensibility or will power.

'Will you come now, Jo?' asked Sam happily.

'I have a few things still to see to here, so I think it would be best if you go on to visit Chrissie. Later on, after I've finished packing and rung my sister, I could . . . when . . .' She looked at Jake. 'When will you be back?'

'Probably about four o'clock,' he replied.

'We're having lunch in a rest . . . rest . . . What is it, Uncle Jake?' Sam frowned.

'A restaurant,' he answered patiently.

'In a restaurant, Jo. Won't that be fun? Are you sure you can't come, too?' she appealed to Jo again.

'No. No, I don't think so. I'll come over when you get home.'

Jake reached into his pocket and unclipped a key from his keyring. 'Here, take the key to the house. You can go over and get settled in when you're ready.'

His fingers touched hers as he put the key into her hand, and Jo stood up abruptly, a sinking feeling gnawing at the pit of her stomach, the icy cold key burning her hand. It was all settled.

After they left Jo sat composing her phone call to her stepsister, and taking a deep breath, she forced herself to dial the number.

'Maggie? It's Jo.'

'Jo!' Maggie yelled into the receiver, forcing Jo to hold the earpiece inches from her ear. 'Thank heavens!

I'd about convinced myself that something horrendous had happened to you. Has the phone been out of order? I haven't been able to raise you and short of ringing at dead of night . . . If Ben hadn't needed the car today I'd have been on your doorstep.'

As Maggie paused for breath Jo managed to get a few words in. 'I tried to ring you, too. I suppose you were over at Ben's parents' place.'

'Yes. The night before last we were.'

'How are they?' Jo played for time.

'They're fine. But what about you? Was it the phone or did you go out both nights?' Maggie persisted.

'I . . . went out. To dinner,' Jo said slowly.

'Out to dinner!' Maggie's voice rose excitedly. 'You did? Jo, that's wonderful! I knew the cottage would work wonders for you. Where did you go? In to Tweed Heads or did you go south?'

'No, not exactly. I . . . Well, the people next door, in the old O'Connor place, they invited me over, so I . . . I went.'

There was a slight pause while Maggie took that in. 'Did you enjoy it?'

'Yes. They're . . . nice people,' Jo said lamely.

'Oh, Jo, you don't know how happy that makes me. It's a big step in the right direction.' Maggie sighed. 'I'm glad. Who are they? Tell me all.'

'There's not a lot to tell really. I don't know that much about them.'

'Well, how long have they been there? I didn't see any sign of them last time we were down.'

'As far as I know they've been there a couple of months. Jake . . . he knew you and Ben owned the cottage.' Jo hoped Maggie hadn't noticed her slip.

'He did?' Maggie's voice held surprise. 'I wonder how? Perhaps old Mr Warren at the real estate agency mentioned it. He's a bit of an old gossip.'

'That must have been it.' Jo was relieved.

'Who's Jake?' asked Maggie, making short work of Jo's rush of relief.

'Jake?' she repeated, trying to sound offhand and only succeeding in appearing flustered. 'He owns the house.'

'Is he married?' Maggie asked over-casually.

'I . . . no, I don't think so.'

'Oh.' There was a wealth of expression in that word and Jo felt herself flush. 'Is he tall, dark and handsome as well as unmarried?' Maggie sounded amused.

'Yes, I guess you could say that,' Jo replied drily. Too tall, dark and handsome for his own good.

'How about rich?' laughed Maggie. 'What does he do for a living?'

'I really couldn't say.'

'Oh. You said "they". Does he live with his parents?' Maggie delved.

'No. There's a housekeeper called Chrissie, or at least there was. She had an accident yesterday and broke her leg. That's why I was over there again last night. I . . . I stayed with Jake's niece until he arrived home from the city.'

'There's a niece, too?'

'Yes. Her name's Samantha and she's six.' Jo closed her eyes and gripped the edge of the breakfast bar.

'I see.' Maggie's voice had softened. 'Why's she staying with her uncle?'

'Her parents were . . . killed last year. I don't know much about it, but what I actually rang you to tell you was that with Chrissie in hospital there's no one to look after Sam, so I . . . I said I would. Just for a few weeks.'

There was an astonished silence on the other end of the line.

'Maggie? Are you still there?'

'Yes, I'm here. I don't know what to say, Jo. How

'. . . will you be able to manage?' Maggie asked soberly.

'I think so.' The dull ache had returned to the region of Jo's heart. 'She's a nice little thing and I don't think she'll be any trouble.'

'But what about you, Jo? I know how you feel about—well,' Maggie paused, searching for the right words.

'I'll be fine, Maggie. I'm . . . there doesn't appear to be anyone else to help out,' Jo finished lamely. 'I couldn't exactly refuse.' That was true enough. With Jake Marshall using his persuasive powers plus a smattering of emotional blackmail she hadn't stood a chance.

'If you're sure, then,' said Maggie, 'and for what it's worth I think it's a marvellous idea. You will keep me posted, though, won't you?'

'Of course. I'll ring and let you know the Marshalls' phone number when I move over there.'

'You mean you're going over to stay there?' Maggie asked. 'At their house?'

'Yes, Jake thinks that would be best.' Jo felt a twinge of irritation at her complacency.

'Jo?'

'Yes?'

'Does he know about—I mean, does he know who you are?' Maggie asked quietly.

'Yes, he recognised me from the advertisements. I'd better go now. I've a bit of tidying to do before I drive over to the house. Say hello to Ben and the girls.'

'Okay, Jo, and if you want to talk or anything—well, you know where I am, love.'

'Thanks, Maggie. Goodbye.' Jo slowly replaced the receiver and sat down on the kitchen stool resting her chin on her hands. She had told Maggie that she would be all right, that she would be able to cope. A prickling of dread invaded her and she felt herself tense involuntarily. How she hoped she was right!

Eventually there was nothing left for her to do to postpone her departure, and she put her two small cases into the Mini and headed over to the house. There was no car parked in the open garage and feeling something of a trespasser Jo walked up to the door and fitted the key into the lock.

It didn't take her long to unpack and, glancing at her watch, she decided to organise the evening meal. She had taken on the job, so she might as well make a start. Her head was in the refrigerator as she was taking stock of its contents when the pealing of the phone startled her so badly that she almost up-ended the tray of meat she was holding. She stood poised for some seconds before she forced herself to move.

'Hello.' Jo's knuckles were white where they clasped the receiver.

'It's Jake Marshall here.'

At the sound of his voice, its tone even deeper through the earpiece, Jo's legs began to shake and she groped behind her for a chair. 'Oh, yes. Hello,' she said weakly.

'I wanted to make sure you'd arrived okay and to tell you not to worry about dinner. Sam and I are almost home and we've picked up some take-aways. I hope you like Chinese food?'

'Yes, I do. Thank you,' Jo was finding trouble catching her breath.

'Fine, we'll see you in about half an hour. And Jo,' his voice dropped lower, 'thanks again for agreeing to help us out.'

It was some time before Jo could rouse herself sufficiently to tear her unseeing gaze from the now silent telephone.

CHAPTER SIX

THAT first morning Jo woke early, the sun streaming in through the open curtains on the window, and she turned in the unfamiliar bed, blinking a couple of times before she was able to place the pastel blue room. Jake Marshall. She was at his house and would be for some time. Closing her eyes tightly, she forcibly calmed her suddenly racing heartbeats.

The whole house was silent save for an occasional friendly creak of settling timber in the warming framework. Sighing, Jo turned over to snuggle down in the bed, but a noise from the kitchen had her sitting bolt upright. Should she get up to see who it was? She didn't want to encounter Jake Marshall, that was for sure. But what if it was Sam?

Jo threw back her bedclothes and reached for her long terry-towelling robe. Pulling it around her, she tied the belt at her waist as she walked quickly over to her door and slowly pulled it open, moving hesitantly along the hall towards the kitchen.

She was halfway across the dining room when a muffled oath halted her steps, and she stood poised. Obviously it was Jake Marshall, and he didn't sound to be in a very good mood. Perhaps he was one of those people who were out of sorts first thing in the morning. Mike had been like that. Just the slightest noise could provoke a tirade of ill-humoured words. Jo had always manoeuvred herself and Jamie out of his way until he had settled down.

As she hovered uncertainly Jake appeared in the doorway, his hair ruffled as though he had been running his hands through it. His chin was dark with his unshaven beard and his eyes looked heavy and tired. He was fully dressed in the same clothes he had been wearing the day before, although he had unbuttoned his shirt almost to his waist and it fell open to show his tanned chest with its light covering of dark hair.

Surely he hadn't been working all night? Jo remembered hearing the faint clicking of his typewriter as she drifted off to sleep. He stopped as he caught sight of her, his coffee cup halfway to his mouth.

'Good morning. I . . .' Jo swallowed, 'I heard a noise and thought it might be Sam.'

He shook his head tiredly and raised the cup of coffee to his lips, taking a gulp and sighing pleasurably. 'I needed that,' he said with feeling. 'How about a cup? The water's hot.'

'Yes, I would like one.' Jo walked forward, her body tense as Jake turned back into the kitchen and she followed him in.

Setting his own cup on the countertop, he reached for another cup and spooned in the coffee grains before she could voice an offer to make her own. He held the steaming mug out to her, handle first, and she took it from him.

'Thank you.' Her hands wrapped about the mug's warmth.

They stood in a lengthening silence sipping their coffee, and although Jo's eyes remained fixed on the mug in her hand she felt Jake's gaze rove over her multiplying her growing tension. Unable to bear the silence any longer, she nervously raised her eyes.

'Have you . . . you didn't work all night, did you?' she asked.

He grimaced. 'I scarcely noticed the time until the sun began to shine through the window.' He flexed his shoulders stiffly. 'I'm pleased with what I've done, though. I achieve much more if I work while I'm in the mood, and lately, I haven't had time to let the mood grab me.'

'You must be tired,' Jo remarked inadequately, and he grinned lopsidedly.

'That I am.' His eyes moved over her face to settle on her lips and Jo felt herself begin to tremble inside. 'Come on through to the study. It's more comfortable in there.' He didn't wait for her acquiescence but turned and motioned for her to precede him out of the kitchen.

The sleeve of her robe brushed his bare arm as she moved past him and it was all she could do to keep her footsteps even and unhurried while all her agitated foresight screamed for her to burst into a frenzied race away from him.

'What exactly do you write?' she asked him as she stood eyeing the neat pile of typing paper and the typewriter with one piece of paper still held in it.

He didn't reply, and she turned to him, her eyebrow raised enquiringly. A puzzled look flashed momentarily into his eyes and he took another sip of his coffee before he answered. 'Books,' he said.

'You mean you're an author?' Jo asked in surprise, somehow seeing him as a journalist.

His face broke into a grin then, adding a certain boy-ishness to his angular handsomeness. 'You could say that.' The amusement continued to play about his mouth.

'What kind of books do you write? I can't say I've . . .' Jo stopped, flushing with embarrassment.

'Heard of me,' he finished. 'I don't write under my own name.' He motioned to the bookshelf to the side of his desk and Jo set her cup of coffee on the desktop before stepping across to take one of the books he indicated from the uniform collection on one shelf.

Her hand began to tremble and she gasped in disbelief. 'You mean you're Jason Marsh?' she asked incredulously.

He inclined his head before draining his coffee cup.

'But I've read just about all of your books. At least,
up until the ... I ... I thoroughly enjoyed them.
They're great!' She looked up at him, reading scep-
ticism in his sardonic look. 'Really,' she said honestly.

Setting his cup aside, he stepped around the desk.
'Thank you.'

At his nearness Jo's nerves began to clamour for
space and she wished she could move away from him
without inviting a look of knowing mockery.

'I've seen all your plays,' he said quietly, and Jo's
entire body stiffened. 'And I enjoyed them too.'

Jo's fingers had tightened on the book she held and
he lifted his hand, his fingers covering hers, feeling
their tension, and he gently prised the book from her
grasp.

'Your last play had my preference,' he said as Jo
relinquished his book.

As he replaced the book on the shelf her fingertips
found the ridged scar and when he turned back his
eyes followed her unconscious well remembered journey of torment down the side of her face. All the old
fears, the terror, returned to twist within her and the
desire to let it all tumble in on her to allow herself to
sink into the blackness, the comfort of oblivion very
nearly overcame her.

Don't think! Don't think! she screamed at herself,
and she swung away from his searching eyes to make
her escape. If she could get to her room ...

Strong fingers closed on her arm, stayed her flight,
pulled her back around to face him. His other hand
moved up and clasped her hand firmly, taking it away
from her face, and she let her head fall forward in an
automatic gesture so that her hair shielded her cheek
from his eyes. His hands released her only to slide
beneath the curtain of fair hair that shone like spun
gold, backlit by the sunlight now pouring through the

study window. Gently but firmly his thumbs forced
her chin upwards until her eyes met his.

'You are a very fine actress,' he said evenly.

'Are?' Jo's voice caught on the word, her lips twisting bitterly, and she gulped a steadying breath. 'Joelle
Brent is gone, Mr Marshall.'

'Has she?' he asked softly. 'I don't think so. Maybe
she's down for the count, but I admit Joelle Brent
would never have given in the way you have.'

Jo stared up at him as the familiar pain began to
throb deep within her. 'Given in?' she repeated. 'What
do you mean?'

'Just what I said. You won't let the real Joelle Brent
out to fight. Isn't that it, Jo?' he asked quietly his fingers
still imprisoning her, his eyes not surrendering hers.

'No.' It came out as a whisper, almost indiscernible.
'No.' This time she spoke louder, her voice stronger,
and her anger rose to rush over her. 'How could you
know . . .' Tears caught in her throat to choke off her
words, and as her eyes filled his features began to blur
and she had to blink him back into a watery focus.

There was a tenseness in the set of his chin, the line
of his sensuous mouth and his eyelids were half closed,
shadowing his expression. The moment, frozen by the
spark of physical attraction that held them immobile,
became immeasurable, and Jake slowly lowered his lips
to hers, his hands sensually caressing her jawline, her
earlobes, his body moulding itself to hers, barely
touching her, but searing her with its potent maleness.

As his lips took hers Jo was lost. She responded
without conscious hesitation. Her lips parted beneath
his, welcoming his sensuous plundering almost feverishly, as though she was parched with thirst and he
offered her cooling crystal clear water.

Her hands stole around his waist, her body curving
submissively responsive against his, the hard pressure
of his thighs firing her through the soft terry-towelling

of her bathrobe. His fingers were playing down the length of her backbone, his lips trailing from her lips to the velvety whiteness of her throat, and she moaned softly, her fingers moving to twist into the thick blackness of his hair.

Against the solidness of his chest her breasts hardened, throbbed her arousal, and his hands slid lower over her hips to pull her impossibly closer, leaving her in no doubt about his own arousal.

In those searing sensual seconds a small part of Jo realised they had both completely lost their heads, but even though the warning bells clanged loudly for her she disregarded them completely, moving her body against his in an unconsciously alluring surrender.

'Jo? Jo?' A small voice penetrated her spinning mind and brought her back onto an even keel with an almost painful abruptness. 'Jo, where are you?'

Jo stiffened in Jake's arms, her hands sliding to his waist to push away from him. Even as their bodies parted their lips still clung together, disinclined to surrender the moment. As Jake's lips reluctantly released hers his hands slid up her arms to hold her face, his fingers tangling in her hair. His eyes, still dark with his arousal, burnt down into hers, holding her gaze with their intensity.

'The name's Jake,' he said softly.

Jo stared back at him, the tip of her tongue moistening her lips still throbbing from his kisses, the movement an unknowing invitation.

'Say it!' he groaned raggedly. 'My name. I have to hear you say it.'

'Jake,' she whispered.

His hold on her tightened painfully before he put her away from him with just about brutal brusqueness and turned to stride around his desk to seat himself behind his typewriter.

'Jo? Oh, there you are.' Sam's pyjama-clad figure

ran across the carpet to wind her arms around Jo's waist. 'I thought you'd gone away or that I'd dreamed you'd come to stay.'

'No, I'm not a dream,' Jo said softly, trying to slow her accelerating heartbeats.

'Morning, Uncle Jake.' Sam grinned happily at her uncle oblivious of the tension that still had hold of him. 'Are you going to come down on the beach with us today?'

Jake's hand moved tiredly around the back of his neck, massaging his taut muscles. 'I'm afraid not, Sam. I think I'll have a shower and get back to work.' He lifted the sheet of paper in the typewriter and began to scan the half page he had written, his attention focused on it, and Jo turned Sam towards the door.

'Let's get you some breakfast,' she said softly. Jake's dismissal of them had been obvious, but as she moved towards the door she felt a quiver of reawakened sensation down her spine as though his eyes broodingly followed her across the room.

The next few days settled into a routine and Jo found herself feeling better than she had during all the months since the accident. She had little time for thought and she spent a lot of her day on the beach with Sam, who rarely stopped talking. They had set themselves the task of weeding what had once been a fairly large vegetable garden beside the garage, and if it had been left to Sam they would have checked the carefully planted seeds half-hourly.

There was little housework to be done as Chrissie had been meticulously clean, so it was easy for Jo and the child to get out of the house. And away from Jake Marshall. Since that first morning she had barely set eyes on him. He was true to his word and appeared to work from dawn till dusk and well into the night, if the tapping of his typewriter was anything to go by.

Jo reasoned with herself that to keep out of his way

would be her safest bet, because she knew she couldn't trust herself where he was concerned. If she could only take Sam over to the cottage she wouldn't have to face him—but when she tentatively broached the idea on her second day at the house he had flatly refused to discuss it, striding off to his study with his face as black as thunder.

As far as the child was concerned Jo found she could now relax enough to talk calmly to her and even touch her without experiencing her earlier revulsion. She was even sleeping better, despite Jake Marshall's disturbing presence, and now found she could get through the night without waking in the enveloping darkness to a tumbling sensation of pure terror.

About a week later Jo was standing ironing the few clothes she had washed that morning, taking advantage of the hour or so that Sam slept in the afternoon. Subconsciously she listened to the faint sound of Jake's typewriter, wondering at the plot of his latest novel. She would have liked to have asked him about it, but that would mean entering his study alone, and after their encounter on that first morning she always ensured that Sam was with her. To infringe on his domain without Sam would be fraught with all manner of emotional dangers. That Jake was aware of her use of the child as a shield against him was so totally obvious in the partly humorous partly ironic expression in his dark blue eyes when they caught hers.

The ringing of the telephone made her jump, guiltily aware that her thoughts had been with Jake once again. Hastily she set the iron on its stand and flicked the off switch before dashing for the receiver before it disturbed the household.

'Hel . . . Hello,' she said breathlessly.

There was a short pause before a husky voice demanded if that was Jake Marshall's residence.

'Yes, it is,' Jo replied, not caring for the tone in the woman's voice.

'Who's that speaking?' queried the voice. 'And where's Chrissie?'

'I'm afraid Mrs Christiansen has had a slight accident. She slipped and unfortunately broke her leg. I'm ... I'm Jo Harrison. I'm filling in for her until she's back on her feet.'

'I see. Well, I'd like to speak to Jake,' ordered the voice.

Jo hesitated. 'I'm afraid Mr Marshall's working and has left instructions that he doesn't wish to be disturbed.'

'That doesn't include me. He'll speak to me,' the husky voice dropped lower, exuding self-confidence.

'I'm sorry. Perhaps I could take a message and Ja ... Mr Marshall,' she grimaced at her slip over his name, 'Mr Marshall can ring you back when he's free.' Jo felt terrible having to say it, but Jake had been adamant. In fact that had been all he had said at breakfast after gulping a cup of coffee and disappearing back into his study. No interruptions whatsoever. Both Jo and Sam had been all but tiptoeing about all morning.

There was a moment's heavy silence.

'Who did you say you were?' Gone was the soft huskiness, leaving a thin sharpness.

'Jo Harrison.'

'Yes. Well, Miss Harrison, I suggest you go and inform Mr Marshall that I'm calling. Tell him it's Miss Vale.'

Jo hesitated again. The sound of Jake's typewriter had ceased, but he had made a point of impressing on her that he wasn't to be disturbed. And recalling the black look on his face she suspected he wasn't in the best of moods today.

'Miss Harrison!' The girl did not disguise her irritation.

'Mrs Harrison,' Jo put in, in an effort to play for time.

'Whoever you are I'd advise you to put me through to Jake at once!'

'Who are you talking to, Jo?' asked Sam, walking into the room sleepily rubbing her eyes.

Covering the mouthpiece, Jo whispered, 'Miss Vale.'

'Lexie? Ugh!' said Sam expressively, wrinkling her little nose.

Jo knew she should chastise the child, but somehow she felt more inclined to giggle.

'Mrs Harrison!' The voice rose angrily in Jo's ear. 'I demand that you inform your employer that I'm calling or else I warn you, your job will be on the line!'

Jo sighed. Whichever way she was going to tread on somebody's toes. If this girl was Jake Marshall's fiancée . . . A cold band tightened about the vicinity of her heart, but she forced herself to put it from her. If Lexie Vale was Jake's fiancée surely he would want to make an exception in her case.

'Would you hold the line, please, Miss Vale.' Jo carefully put down the receiver and walked towards the study.

'Uncle Jake's going to be mad as mad,' warned Sam in a voice of doom.

Jo raised her hands and let them fall in a gesture of resignation and walked on to the study door. Taking a deep breath, she knocked softly. The sound of the typewriter never missed a beat and Jo knocked again. The typing stopped and what sounded like a muffled oath preceded a short call for her to enter.

'There's a phone call for you,' Jo began, not at all encouraged by the dark scowl on Jake's face.

'No calls,' he said shortly, his eyes reverting dismissingly to the typed sheet in front of him.

'It's Miss Vale.' Jo remained hovering by the open door.

His eyes flicked to her and back to the typewriter. 'Tell her to ring back next week.'

'I don't think she's going to take that from me,' Jo said quietly.

'Why not?'

'Why should she? She doesn't know me from Adam.'

He shrugged. 'Just tell her to ring back.' Barely disguising his irritation, he glanced up at her again, his eyebrows lifting enquiringly when Jo continued to stand there. 'What is it now?'

'Well, being your fiancée . . .' Jo stopped as his brows drew together.

'Did Lexie tell you that?'

'No, not exactly. It was Sam.'

'Sam?'

Jo nodded, and he gave her a level look before standing up and striding around the desk.

'Then I'd best not blot my copybook by keeping my——' he paused, 'fiancée waiting.'

Sam watched her uncle dubiously as he strode across to pick up the telephone, her face breaking into a grin when he winked at her. Jo wondered if she should leave the room instead of continuing with her ironing. However, had Jake wanted privacy for his call surely he would have taken it on the extension in the study. She'd simply just have to close her ears.

'Hello, Lexie. Jake here.'

To shut out Jake's deep voice was easier said than done, and no matter how hard she tried Jo found herself listening to his every word. Not that he said very much. Lexie Vale appeared to be doing the majority of the talking.

Only when Jake turned slightly back towards her did Jo drop her eyes to the small dress of Sam's she was preparing to press.

'Actually Mrs Harrison has been a great help stepping into the beach,' Jake was saying, and at the mention of her name Jo glanced up at him to catch a flash of amusement in his eyes. 'Well, no, not quite of Chrissie's vintage, but you wouldn't call her a teenager.'

Jo flushed angrily. How dared he discuss her with some else as though she wasn't there!

'Very attractive,' commented Jake into the mouthpiece, his eyes dancing over Jo's figure, and Sam smothered a giggle with a dimpled hand.

'We haven't discussed that.' Jake's voice had sharpened and he turned away from Jo, shoving his hand into the side pocket of his jeans, rocking backwards and forwards on the balls of his feet the muscles of his thighs flexing, as he listened frowningly to what Lexie had to say.

'Sorry, Lexie,' he said at last. 'Can't make it. I'm going to be working flat out for at least a fortnight, maybe longer if I get any interruptions.'

His frown deepened as he cast a quick glance back at Jo. 'I told you last week I was going to be working. I have a deadline to meet, so it's no go.' A few seconds later he replaced the receiver and by the look on his face his parting had not been amicable. Jo looked quickly down at her ironing.

'That was Lexie, wasn't it, Uncle Jake? She's not coming down here, is she?' asked Sam bluntly.

'Don't think so,' replied Jake evenly, and stretched languidly. 'What I need now to clear the cobwebs is a swim. Have I got any takers?'

'Me!' squealed Sam. 'I'll get my togs on.' She ran out of the room.

'How about it, Jo?' He stood with arms folded, looking so disturbingly masculine that she had to drag her eyes from him.

'No, I think I'll finish this,' she said quickly, her eyes lifting to his face as he walked across the carpet towards her.

'Chicken!' he murmured huskily, his eyes challenging as he stood with feet apart, hands casually on his hips. 'Leave that. It's not imperative that you finish it right now.'

'I know that, but I ... I really don't feel like swimming,' Jo finished lamely.

'You'll enjoy it once you're in the water,' he smiled the smile that turned her legs to jelly. 'Come on, Jo. You know what they say about all work and no play.'

She knew the moment he smiled at her that she would give in to his appeals, and she sighed and switched off the iron once again. 'I'll go and change,' she said as she walked past him.

'Good girl,' he said, his voice deep and vibrant.

Good girl, indeed! Jo fumed to herself as she donned her black bikini. Anyone would think she was Sam's age and he was patting her on the head because she was doing as she was told. If the truth were known he most probably wanted her along to mind Sam so that he could have a free-and-easy dip in the surf. And she, of course, had played right into his manipulating hands.

She bit her lip as her thoughts went off at a tangent with her choice of adjectives. Manipulating hands. Her mind conjured up a vivid picture of Jake's hands moving assuredly over her body, and she sat down heavily on her bed as her legs shook beneath her.

Heavens she thought, she was behaving like a naïve adolescent weaving dreams of knights in shining armour waiting to whisk her away on a tide of perfectly romantic movie-style lovemaking. Her lips clamped tightly together. Well, that was all a smooth celluloid dream. Life had taught her that, if it had taught her nothing else. And these illusory daydreams she could so easily interweave with Jake Marshall proved her fallibility within herself. She was her own worst enemy.

Pushing all these thoughts to the back of her mind, she donned her beach wrap and collected her towel. She knew she must keep the door to her emotions firmly closed and locked on the emptiness inside her. It was her only protection.

Apart from one concise all-encompassing glance when she first joined them Jake barely acknowledged her presence, making no effort to talk to either her or the child as they walked down on to the beach. In brief dark blue swim shorts, his towel slung carelessly over one shoulder, he looked simply magnificent and so compellingly masculine. So much so that Jo was hard pressed to keep her mind on Sam's happy chatter as she skipped along between the two adults.

Standing selfconsciously fingering the tie belt of her robe, Jo breathed a sigh of relief as Jake dropped his towel in a heap on the soft warm white sand and strode straight down to the surf where the waves were only moderately high as the light wind was blowing offshore. Sam ran after her uncle, gaily calling Jo as she went.

The water was almost painfully cold to Jo's sand-warmed bare feet and she shivered as the waves splashed her legs. But both Jake and the child seemed oblivious of the cold as they plunged enthusiastically into the turquoise water.

'Come on, Jo,' encouraged Sam. 'It's really warm once you get under.'

Gingerly Jo used her cupped hand to wet her dry body in the hope that the water wouldn't seem so cold, all the while aware of Jake's tanned body floating easily, his eyes watching her with amusement.

'Would it be any easier if Sam and I helped you in?' he asked, chuckling teasingly.

'No, thanks,' Jo hastily assured them. 'I prefer to do it in my own time.'

'Oh, me too! But sometimes it's more fun with a

little help from a friend,' he remarked outrageously, and struck out towards her.

That settled it as far as Jo was concerned. Taking a quick breath, she dived into the oncoming wave, surfacing some distance away to flick her wet hair back out of her face, her eyes searching for Jake's tanned body.

His deep laugh came from her right. 'I told you all you needed was a little help.'

Before Jo could reply Sam's arms wrapped about her shoulders and she turned to the child in surprise. 'How did you get out here?' she asked. Jo could only just touch bottom, so there was no way Sam could.

'I swam,' replied Sam proudly. 'I'm a really good swimmer, aren't I, Uncle Jake? I've been swimming all my life. Watch me ride into the beach on the next wave!'

No sooner had she said it than her little body had gone, her head bobbing along with the beach-bound wave.

'Will she be all right?' Jo asked Jake worriedly, not taking her eyes off Sam's head for fear of losing sight of her.

'Yes. She can swim like a fish.' Jake was much closer now, treading water as the waves lifted their feet from the sandy sea floor. 'But I still keep an eye on her, of course. She's confident in the water, but not fool-hardy.'

As they both watched her Sam stood up out of the foam where the sea had deposited her on the beach and she turned to wave to them, her face creased in a huge smile.

'I'm going to build a sand castle,' she called out to them, and began to dig into the sand on the water's edge.

Feeling Jake beside her, Jo turned to look at him. 'It's not so cold once you're wet, after the initial shock, that is,' she said breathily, liking the way the droplets of salty water running from his tanned shoulders glistened like diamonds in the sunlight.

He was watching her too, his eyes sliding over her now warm body. 'You'll have to take care you don't get sunburnt. Your skin's quite fair.'

'As long as I don't grossly overdo it, I tan quite well without burning. I'm lucky, I guess.'

A large swell lifted them and Jo spread her arms out to steady herself, keeping her chin high of the water. Jake had done the same, his hand touching her, his fingers closing around her arm near her elbow. As the wave replaced them on the firmness of the sand his fingers slid over her skin, his thumb probing a slight indentation, and he lifted her arm clear of the water to gaze down at the jagged three-inch scar.

'The same accident?' he asked quietly, his fingers smoothing the mark on the inside of her arm as his eyes met hers.

'Yes.' Jo's hand went up to cover her cheek, but he caught hold of it halfway there, holding it down.

'I know the scar on your cheek is there, Jo. There's no reason to cover it,' he said evenly, his eyes going deliberately to the side of her face and she flinched slightly, unable to control the involuntary reaction.

His mouth tightened as he lifted her hand again and for a heart-stopping moment she thought he would carry it to his lips.

A wave came upon them unnoticed and, unprepared Jo staggered, clutching at the hands that held hers to steady herself. Jake had also lost his footing and as he went over he pulled Jo with him. Their near-naked bodies brushed together and the sensuousness of that electrifying sensation as they rolled together in the caressing surf made Jo weakly slide her arms about Jake's waist with all the reverent relief of a storm-battered ship finding a safe harbour.

As they surfaced, reality returned and she went to

push away from him, but he held her fast, his arms
locked behind her back, his hands sliding with aesthetic
savour over her water-oiled skin. Their eyes met, held,
drank from their respective depths, his the deep blue
of mid-ocean and hers almost the colour of the turquoise ocean flowing about them.

Jake's body moved against hers, one bare leg in-
sinuating itself between hers, his hands settling low on
her hips, his arousal sparking and kindling an answering fire deep within her.

'Jake, please . . .' Jo began, her voice catching in her
throat.

'That's what I aim to do,' he whispered huskily.
'Please you and go on pleasing you. It's going to give
me great pleasure.' One corner of his mouth lifted in a
crooked smile.

'That's not what I meant. I . . . I want to go back to
the beach.' Jo's palms were flat against his chest, and
she was fighting a burning desire to run her fingers
over the solidness of his chest.

'So do I.' He groaned intensely, his lips brushing
her wet shoulder, his tongue sending a burning fire
raging through her body.

'Jake!' His name came out raggedly. 'Please don't
touch me.'

He raised his head, his arms not releasing her. 'I
want you, Jo,' he said softly, sensually, his voice an
inciting melody with the sounds of the insinuative sea
sighing an accompaniment.

Her breath caught chokingly in her chest as his eyes
seemed to hold her motionless.

'God, can't you feel what you're doing to me, what
you've done to me from the moment I set eyes on you?'
The last part of his question was almost lost to her as
his head came down, shadowing her face from the sun,
and Jo knew she simply wouldn't have had the willpower to deny him that kiss, but lost in each other as

they were, another larger wave suddenly crashed heavily against them, breaking Jake's hold on her as they both sank beneath the water, rolled over by the turbulence of the capricious dumper.

When Jo struggled to the surface, dashing the stinging saltiness from her eyes, she was alone and Jake was moving away from her, his arms moving rhythmically in a powerful crawl. With a hundred mixed and conflicting emotions she let herself drift in to the shore to join Sam, who was happily intent on saving the walls of her castle from the relentless erosion of the incoming tide.

Shading her eyes with her hand, Jo watched Jake's figure out in the water. He had said he wanted her. Quite a number of men had said just that in the old days and had never stirred her to reciprocation. A shiver of fear passed over her and she wrapped her arms about herself. Now she knew what those words meant, for she wanted Jake, too, and she didn't know how to dampen the fire that he had kindled within her, that could so easily rage out of control to consume her.

CHAPTER SEVEN

As the days passed the heightened tension that existed between Jo and Jake seemed to have intensified, grew more explosively volatile each time their paths crossed. And it appeared to Jo that their paths crossed far more frequently than they had done in the days before their encounter in the surf.

Once again Jo's sleep became broken and disturbed, but the disturbance was of a totally different nature from the terror that had relentlessly plagued her in the long dark months after her accident. The reason for her restlessness was an entirely tangible thing. Now it was Jake Marshall who kept her awake, tossing until the small hours of the morning, who set her body throbbing until she wrapped her arms tightly about herself, aching for him, wishing she could run to him, wanting the right to have him kiss her, caress her, carry her to the ultimate satisfaction her no longer dormant body craved.

She knew how often his eyes settled on her, darkly brooding, not even trying to disguise his wanting in their dusky depths, and she only had to picture that look for her body to burn with equal fire. Valiantly she tried to ignore what she read in every line of his tensed, so potent maleness.gh. All she had to do now was to get down to the yacht and conceal herself there without anyone being aware of her absence. A Hehat Jo knew had to break before too long. And it crossed her mind that the most sensible thing to do was to talk it over with Jake, bringing it out into the open before the situation got out of hand and exploded with who knew what result. That was

the sensible thing to do, Jo told herself. But she somehow was unable to even try to broach the subject, with
Jake.

Eventually, Sam's own inkling that all might not be
well between the two adults became the first chink in
the torrid wall of intensity that they had erected. After
lunch one day Jo and Sam were busy making gingerbread men when Jake joined them, standing leaning
easily in the kitchen doorway, long denim-clad legs
crossed at the ankle, arms folded across his broad chest,
the hard watchfulness of his eyes belying his casual
stance.

'What are you two up to?' he addressed them.

Sam looked up from her position kneeling on a kitchen chair, her hands full of red cherries, and smiled
happily across at him. 'We're making gingerbread men
and I'm putting on their red noses. Come and see,
Uncle Jake.'

Jake straightened with the lithe and subtle grace of a
prowling jaguar and stepped across to the table to stand
only feet from Jo's tensed body. 'Will they taste as good
as they look?' he asked, his question directed at his
niece although his tone had Jo's nerves jangling stri-
dently.

'Course they will,' Sam assured him confidently.
'Jo's a fantastic cook. You know, I think Jo and
Chrissie are the bestest cooks in the world.'

Jake raised one eyebrow as his eyes turned to Jo and
her hand holding a beaker of raisins they'd picked out
for the eyes shook perceptibly. His sharp eyes were
not unaware of the fact and his mouth tightened
cruelly.

'Look at these, Uncle Jake!' Sam chatted gaily. 'Jo
put our names on these gingerbread men. See—that
one says "Sam" and that one says "Jo" and this one's
got "Jake" on it. That's yours,' she grinned.

At that moment Jo dropped the cup of raisins from

her nerveless fingers and the raisins tipped out on to
the table, the plastic cup rolling to land on the floor
with a muffled clatter. Both Jo and Jake reached down
simultaneously to retrieve the cup and Jo felt his warm
breath fan her cheek. When his fingers touched hers
she snatched her hand away as though she had been
burned, a quickly bitten off gasp escaping her lips.

Straightening up immediately, Jake looked dark with
anger, the fallen cup forgotten, and slowly Jo stood up
beside him, her face flushed.

'When it's cooked Jo can eat mine. It should give
her the utmost satisfaction,' he said gruffly as he strode
out of the room.

Jo stood staring at the empty doorway through
which he had disappeared, and only when Sam touched
her arm did she drag herself back out of her shocked
immobility. Sam was now standing on the chair, her
plain little face pale, her bottom lip trembling.

'Why's Uncle Jake so mad, Jo? Is he angry with us?'
Two large tears trickled down the child's cheeks.

Involuntarily Jo's arms went about the little girl,
held the soft little body close, taking an unsought comfort from that closeness. 'He's . . . he's not angry with
you, love,' she began, brushing Sam's hair back from
her forehead.

'Then is he mad at you?' This thought upset the
little girl even more and she gulped on a sob. 'I don't
want Uncle Jake to be mad at you, Jo.'

'Your uncle's just tired. You know how hard he's
been working on his book and because he's tired he's a
little short-tempered.' Jo hoped she sounded more
convincing than she felt.

'You won't go away, will you, Jo?' Sam's arms
clutched fiercely around Jo's neck almost desperately.
'Even if Uncle Jake's mad, you won't go away and
leave us, will you?'

Jo's heart contracted painfully at the worried look

on Sam's face and she reached up to wipe the tears from the child's face with her hand. 'Now how can I possibly leave when we've all these gingerbread men to cook?' She forced a brightness into her voice, wondering with a sinking ache within her what she could be doing to this innocent, insecure little scrap. For eventually she would have to hand them back, Jake and Sam, to Chrissie's ministrations. She swallowed a painful aching in her throat, refusing to allow herself to acknowledge the fact that not only the devastating Jake Marshall but also this child who needed so much love and reassurance had found their way beneath the curtain of her defensive armour.

Although Jo had made light of the whole incident and infused her voice with as much lightness as she could muster she knew that for Sam, as for herself, some of the enjoyment had gone out of the cookie-making project. For the remainder of the afternoon while Jake exiled himself in his study, his typewriter silent, Jo felt the troubled eyes of the child rest on her.

Jake took his dinner in his study as well, and as Jo was reading Sam her ritual bedtime story he appeared in the doorway, his chin darkly shadowed with a day's unshaven beard. Both Jo and Sam looked up at him with a certain amount of misgivings and he grimaced slightly as he came to sit on the bottom of the bed.

'Which story are we reading tonight? Not *The Happy Prince* again?' he asked at last.

'No, *The Voyage of the Poppykettle*. Jo and I borrowed it from the library when we collected the groceries,' Sam told him. 'It's all about some Hairy Peruvians. They're gnomes and they set out to look for a new home. Come and look, Uncle Jake!' She pointed to the book open on Jo's knee.

He stood up and came to stand beside Jo where she sat on the edge of the bed near the child. His jean-clad leg touched Jo's knee and the rasping sound of the thick denim against the cotton of her dress seemed to thunder in her ears.

'Look at their boat, Uncle Jake.' Sam pointed to the illustrations. 'It's a poppykettle, like a teapot, and they're going to sail across the ocean to Australia in it. Aren't they brave?' She turned the pages. 'Here's where the dolphin helps them. Do you want Jo to start at the beginning so you can hear the whole story?' she asked enthusiastically.

'Not tonight. I'll leave you both to it. Besides, it sounds as though Jo has read it more than once already.' He touched Sam on the nose with his finger before leaning across to plant a kiss where his finger had touched, his other hand momentarily resting on Jo's shoulder to steady himself. Then he stepped away and Jo's body seemed to sigh with a mixture of regret and relief.

He flexed his muscles tiredly. 'I really came in to say goodnight. I'll have a shower and get an early night,' he said, stifling a yawn. 'See you both tomorrow.'

'Would you like a cup of tea or coffee before you go?' Jo asked, and he shook his head.

'Why don't you kiss Jo goodnight, too, Uncle Jake?' piped up Sam out of the blue, and Jo's face flushed a deep red. 'Even if you have got tickly whiskers.'

'Why not?' He grinned teasingly and stepped towards them and before Jo realised what he was about he had lifted her hand and planted a quick kiss on her open palm, sending her heartrate sky-high. The touch of his lips on her hand had been almost as charged a sensation as his lips on her mouth would have been.

Sam giggled her goodnight, leaning her cheek against Jo's shoulder as her uncle left them. With resolution Jo collected herself and began to pick up their story, only half her mind on what she was reading.

'There we are,' she finished. 'That's a nice story, isn't it?'

'Mmm. I wish the Hairy Peruvians had landed on our beach.' Sam sighed and looked up at Jo, her brow furrowed. 'Jo, can I ask you something?'

'Of course.' Jo kept her voice level, suddenly knowing she might not be able to handle the question that was about to be put to her.

'Do you like Uncle Jake?' Sam's big blue eyes held Jo's.

'What makes you think I wouldn't like him?' Jo hedged, her throat tightening nervously.

'Oh, I don't know,' Sam shrugged. 'I guess I just want you to like him.'

'Well, I do like him.' Jo straightened the bedclothes as the little girl lay back against her pillow. 'Now, off to sleep.'

'He likes you, Jo—I can tell.'

Jo's face burned again. 'That's good. It's nice to be liked.'

'I don't suppose you'd like to marry him, would you?' Sam asked earnestly. 'Then I could be your little girl as well as Uncle Jake's.'

Jo's heart lurched as she stared down at Sam's solemn little face. 'Oh, Sam,' she said helplessly, sinking back down on the side of the bed. 'Sam, it's not that simple. People ... well, people have to be in love with each other in a special way before even thinking about getting married.'

'I know.' Sam sighed again. 'But do you think you might be able to love Uncle Jake in a special way?'

'I haven't known your uncle very long and we don't really know much about each other,' Jo said lamely, 'so I couldn't really tell you that.'

'Oh.' Sam paused. 'I thought that seeing as Uncle Jake kissed you this morning when we were swimming, he might like to marry you and then you wouldn't go away.' Sam's voice caught on a sob and Jo took hold of her hand.

'You know I'll only be here until Chrissie's leg gets better,' Jo began quietly. 'Then I'll be going back to . . . to the cottage.'

'But I like you, Jo, and I want you to stay for always.' Sam rubbed her eyes.

'We can—well, we can still visit.' Jo felt absolutely lost trying to handle the situation, and the remembered thought that she had known before she had agreed to come that something like this would happen gave her no consolation at all.

Sam gazed up at her, her hands clutching the bed-clothes. 'I still think you should marry Uncle Jake. He's very nice and so are you, Jo. So much nicer than Lexie.' Her eyes fell to her hands. 'Lexie's horrid!'

'Sam, I don't think you should mention all this to your uncle,' Jo said hurriedly, deciding the discussion had gone far enough and imagining her embarrassment if Sam chose to bring up the subject with her uncle in Jo's presence. 'Besides, if your uncle wants to marry Miss Vale you'll just have to accept it. It's his choice.'

Sam gave a heavy sigh and Jo passed her a tissue. 'Come on now, blow your nose and stop worrying. Tomorrow we'll try to make a necklace out of the shells you found on the beach.'

Sam nodded sadly, sniffing against the rolled up tissue as she slid down in the bed. Jo bent down and kissed her and Sam's arms wound around her. ' 'Night, Jo. I love you and Uncle Jake the most in the world.'

Tears glistened on Jo's eyelashes as she went to her own room to collect her nightgown and robe to take to the shower. As she walked soft-footedly along the hall-way she listened carefully for some sound that meant Jake was still awake, but his door was firmly closed and no strip of light showed beneath it. As she stood beneath the warm spray of the shower she could almost laugh at herself. Had Jake been awake what had she planned on doing? She could hardly brazenly knock on his bedroom door and ... She stopped. And what indeed!

Jo's shower did much to relax her aching muscles and she settled into the comfortable bed with a sigh of physical if not conscious tiredness. Of course, sleep didn't come. The mental picture she had of Jake's face, his whole body, seemed to be sketched in an indelible ink to stand between her over-active mind and the peaceful oblivion of slumber.

Sam's words added themselves to the whole tableau and Jo sat up, drawing up her legs, resting her chin on her knees. Marrying Jake Marshall—the very thought brought an aroused anticipation for one unguarded moment before it faded into a bittersweet ache. Jo wiped her hand over her eyes. What could be happening to her? If she didn't know better, if she hadn't closed that part of her life and locked it away making an empty void deep inside her she would have said she was in love with the man. But of course she had. And she wasn't. Was she?

She had all the symptoms—the nerve-honing tension when he was near, the wild racing of her heart when she so much as thought about him, as she was this very minute, with her pulse accelerating like wildfire. And the burning ache when he touched her that left her breathless with wanting him. God, how she wanted him! Wanted him more than she'd ever wanted any other man.

And he had admitted himself that he wanted her too. Jo's arms tightened about her drawn-up legs. Wanting and loving were two totally different emotions. At least she'd always thought so. Now she was so mixed up she scarcely knew what to think. Jake Marshall had thawed her frozen thinking processes and set them spinning, turned that ordered life of hers into an almost unreal, fairytale type of existence. Everything had seemed so cut and dried in her life before the accident.

Now she knew just how easily she could involve herself in an affair with Jake, and she couldn't cope with that, could she? A tiny niggling of doubt tried to tell her she would take anything that Jake offered her, and she squeezed her eyes tightly shut.

Damn Jake Marshall! No man before had even tempted her to consider an affair. Admittedly in the beginning Mike had suggested they live together, have a trial marriage, but Jo had had no trouble deciding against that idea and they had married three months later. She sighed, the pang of guilt that always accompanied thoughts of Mike rising within her. Perhaps if they had lived together they would have realised they were not truly compatible and they would never have married at all. And never had Jamie.

Jamie. Jo's heart lurched. When she had held him in her arms for the first time she had felt such exquisite joy and wonder. He had been so beautiful even then, just minutes after he was born. And she knew she would never forget the tinge of fear that grew with the joy. Fear that she now had the responsibility of his upbringing, fear that she might have to do it alone, because even then she and Mike had grown into total strangers. And the other, more terrible fear that she had forced from her mind the very second she thought it. That Jamie was too beautiful, that she was far too lucky and that somewhere, some time, she would have to pay. Like on a cold black rainy night on a narrow mountain road . . .

No! No! Don't think! Don't think! she screamed at herself, hearing that scream of terror echo in her head so that she covered her ears. It was then she realised that she was not responsible for the screaming, and she was out of bed and along the hall to Sam's room before she remembered instructing her immobile limbs into motion.

Although the night lamp was still burning Jo flicked on the main overhead light and flew across to the bed where the child lay huddled. The bedclothes were in a tangled mess on the floor and Sam had drawn herself into a ball, her face pressed into the mattress muffling her screams just a little.

Reaching out, Jo turned her over and the cries intensified almost chilling her blood. In the babble of sounds the child made one horrific sentence, sharp and clear. 'Mummy's got blood on her dress!' For a second Jo froze and then she was gathering the child against her, rocking her gently back and forth, talking softly, crooning almost, until the screams became sobs and Sam's arms clutched around her, clinging painfully with a desperation that revealed just how terrified the child had been those moments before.

'Come on now, love, stop crying,' Jo soothed. 'I'm here and it's all over.' Sinking down on the bed, she gently wiped the child's damp hair back from her face, her own thin nightdress wet from Sam's perspiration-soaked pyjamas. Well could she understand the terror of the journey that the child had taken in her sleep, and her heart ached for her. She put her lips to Sam's forehead and gently prized the thin little arms from around her neck.

'I'm here, Sam. There's nothing to be afraid of any more.'

'Oh, Jo, I was scared,' Sam gulped. 'Don't leave me! Don't leave me! I'm frightened by myself.'

'There, there.' Jo held Sam's head against her shoulder, laying her cheek on the damp hair, and over the child's head her eyes caught a movement as Jake advanced into the room.

His robe was pulled crookedly around his obviously naked body, his hair tousled, and the paleness of his face suggested he was trying to shrug off the drugging quality of what must have been a deep sleep. He con-

tinued across the room and the bed creaked as he sat
down beside Jo and the child, his added weight pulling
Jo towards him before she could readjust herself to the
slope of the mattress.

His bare leg rested against Jo's and his arm went
across hers to gently rub Sam's head. 'Hey, what's all
this, poppet?' he asked teasingly.

'Oh, Uncle Jake!' Sam looked up at him, her face
pale, her cheeks wet with tears. 'I dreamed again. I
dreamed that terrible dream where Mummy was . . .'
she gulped. 'Oh, Uncle Jake, I was all by myself!' she
finished on a sob, and threw herself at Jake's chest.

'Well, it's all over now. Jo and I are here,' he said
softly as he gathered her into his arms.

After a while the child's sobs subsided and she
yawned tiredly. 'Can I have a drink, please, Uncle
Jake?'

'I'll get her one.' Jo rose and reached for the jug on
the bedside table, filling the mug and carrying it back
to hold it for Sam while she drank thirstily.

'She's sopping wet, and so is the bed,' Jo murmured
softly.

Jake nodded and stood up with Sam in his arms.
'I'll give her a warm bath if you'll change the bed,' he
said as he left the room.

Jo had the bed remade by the time Jake returned
with Sam cosily wrapped in a fluffy bath towel. Jo
quickly dressed the child in fresh dry pyjamas and Sam
lay back on the bed, very nearly asleep again. Pulling
the bedclothes up, Jo tucked her in and smoothed her
hair down, frowning worriedly at the paleness of Sam's
face.

'She'll be all right now,' Jake said quietly.

'But she might wake up again. Hadn't I better sit
with her?'

'No, you go to bed.' Jake ran his hand over his hair
and his robe fell open to the waist. 'She doesn't usually

wake again. She always seems to go off into a sound
undisturbed sleep after these nightmares. But I'll stay
with her for a while to make sure she's settled.'

He switched off the main light and turned back to
Sam, his eyes glinting bright in the semi-darkness, and
Jo was all at once aware of the thinness of her nightdress, made even more transparent by its dampness
and she shivered slightly.

'You're cold. Better get changed as well,' he said
evenly. 'Thanks for seeing to Sam,' he added quietly
as Jo brushed past him and hurried back to her room.

Leaning against her bedroom door, she began to
shake in earnest as the light breeze from the sea blew
in her bedroom window, gently stirring the curtains.
She looked down at herself, horrified at the figure she
made in the semi-transparent nightdress. Heavens, she
might as well have been naked! As he was. Her cheeks
burned as she angrily shrugged the damp material over
her head and reached in her drawer for a fresh nightdress.

She was being absolutely ridiculous, she chastised
herself as she slid back into bed. Both of them had
simply reacted automatically when Sam had started
screaming, springing out of bed with no thoughts of
modesty.

But her thin nightdress had fallen over her body,
highlighting her full breasts and nicely rounded hips
to finish high above her knees, displaying the long
length of her legs. Jo's face flamed as she drew the
sheets belatedly to cover herself, trying to reassure
herself that Jake had seen much more of her body when
she wore her bikini. And he had been far more interested in the child than in Jo's dress, or lack of it.

She recalled the way he had looked at her as she left
him and she squeezed her eyes tightly closed to wipe
out the memories of the fire in the brilliance of his
eyes.

A short time later she heard Jake's quiet tread as he made his way along the hall. Her heart seemed to literally cease beating when his footsteps paused by her door, only to continue past to his own room. After that Jo found it impossible to sleep.

Forcibly keeping thoughts of Jake from her mind, she stared upwards to where the moonlight had found various chinks in her curtains to throw abstract designs on the ceiling. Then her thoughts centred on Sam. What had triggered off the child's nightmare? What horrific sights had she stored away in her young mind that could produce such a terrible dream? Obviously it was all to do with her parents' death. And who could say what had started it all off again?

Jo herself could rarely put her finger on any one thing that became the catalyst that had her waking in the very same manner that Sam had tonight, screaming in terror, nightclothes and bed soaked from her ordeal. The whole thing seemed to build up until one night it ran relentlessly through like a celluloid dream, complete with a graphic authenticity and brilliant, terror-provoking clarity. Her heart went out to the child, so young to be suffering such agonies.

Finally, after tossing restlessly for what seemed like hours, Jo threw back the bedclothes and flicked on her reading lamp. Perhaps a cup of tea would induce sleep. Anything to relieve the soul searching wakefulness she was enduring. Slipping out of bed, she drew on her robe and eased her bedroom door open, sliding through to tiptoe along the hall, leaving her door slightly ajar so that the pale light lit the hallway. She peeped into Sam's room, but the child was sleeping peacefully as though the nightmare had never been. Jo continued on to the kitchen, carefully stepping around the shadowy furniture.

The tea brewed, she sat down at the small kitchen

table and took a sip, sighing as the hot liquid spread it
warmth through her body.

'Sounds like you needed that.' Jake's voice very
nearly frightened her to death and she gazed back at
him, lost for words, as he walked into the kitchen. 'I
could do with a cup myself. May I join you?' Without
waiting for her reply he took a mug off the hook on the
dresser and sat down opposite her.

Jo raised her cup to her lips as he filled his own
mug. All her senses were tinglingly awake now, clamouring at his nearness.

'Trouble sleeping?' he asked after trying his own tea.

Jo nodded. 'I . . . I hoped the cup of tea would do
the trick.'

His eyes roved over her face and Jo swallowed nervously, running her finger around the rim of her cup.

'I guessed as much when I heard you moving about.
It's not easy to relax after being shocked out of a deep
sleep,' he said, and they fell silent, the only sound
coming from the emotionless ticking of the kitchen
clock.

'Does Sam suffer from these nightmares very often?'
Jo asked at last.

'In the beginning she had us up at least once a night,
but she hasn't had one for some time.' He sighed. 'I
had hoped they were behind her, but apparently I was
wrong.' He rubbed his jaw reflectively.

'Have you any idea what might have brought it on?
I mean, did she seem upset or worried about anything
before she went to bed?' he asked.

She was loath to mention his anger of that afternoon,
and noting her hesitation Jake raised an eyebrow enquiringly. Jo shrugged. 'She was a little upset this
afternoon. She thought you were angry with her.'

Jake's eyes flickered and went down to the mug in
his hand. 'I see.'

'But I explained to her that you were tired because

you'd been working so hard and long on your book. As far as I could tell she seemed satisfied with that.'

Jake swore softly and muttered something derisively under his breath. Straining to hear what he said, Jo was sure she had heard him say 'Would that were the truth', and she wondered if perhaps his writing wasn't going as well as he would have liked it to. Then he looked up at her. 'Was that all?'

'Yes,' Jo said hesitantly, and reluctantly felt she had to add, 'She also seems to be worried about your forthcoming marriage to Miss Vale.'

A stillness came over Jake as he slowly took another mouthful of his tea, his eyelids shadowing the expression in his eyes.

'Perhaps you should . . .' Jo stopped, thinking that she could only get into deep water she had no desire to be drawn into if she continued to pursue this subject.

'Should what?' he prompted quietly.

'Well, it appears to me that Sam's very sensitive and maybe a little insecure.' Jo paused. 'What she needs is a mother, so if you explained to her about your—well, your engagement to Miss Vale, let Sam spend more time with your fiancée, get to know her and . . . and like her . . .' Her voice dwindled away and the kitchen clock took over the silence.

'And do you think they would?' Jake asked.

'Would?' Jo repeated incomprehensively.

'Get to like each other.'

'That I couldn't say, as I haven't met Miss Vale,' Jo replied, thinking she didn't care much for her herself if their one telephone conversation was anything to judge the other woman by. 'But surely if they saw more of each other, that would be a start.'

Jake pushed himself away from the table, balancing on the back legs of his chair, and smiled a trifle cynically. 'It's a little more difficult than that. You see, Miss Vale, with no disrespect to her more obvious attractions, is not overly fond of children, Sam in particular, so . . . stalemate.'

Letting his chair fall back with a thud, he folded his arms and leant his elbows on the table, regarding Jo levelly. 'On top of that I'm afraid I'm far too selfish to consider Sam's need for a mother as a reason for deciding to marry.' His eyes burned darkly into hers. 'What can I get out of marriage that I can't have as I am, without taking the plunge?'

Jo felt herself blushing at his candour and tore her eyes from his face. 'I think that's none of my business. My suggestion was simply that—a suggestion, nothing more.'

'I'll accept that, Mrs Harrison,' he said mockingly, inclining his head. 'However, I'd be a callous bastard if I didn't recognise my niece's plight. The poor kid has come through more than a lot of adults could hope to cope with.'

It crossed Jo's mind that the child had coped with her ordeal far better than she had herself, and she pushed the thought away, not wanting to bring it into her mind while Jake Marshall sat opposite her with his ever watchful soul-piercing eyes.

'Chrissie told me both Sam's parents were killed overseas,' Jo remarked to cover her brief distraction.

'You didn't see it in the papers?' Jake asked, and Jo shook her head.

'No. No. I . . . I must have been . . . away at the time,' she said jerkily. How did you tell someone you were most probably lying heavily sedated so you couldn't injure yourself or anyone else? she asked herself bitterly.

'It was about fourteen months ago,' Jake continued. 'The media made the most of it, as usual. Can't blame them, I guess.' He shrugged.

'I believe Chrissie said your brother was a news reporter,' said Jo as she watched his expression harden.

'Through and through.' He grimaced. 'Dave rarely spent more than a couple of weeks in any one place. Even when he came home he'd be itching to get away again. Except for the year he met Denise.' His mouth tightened.

'That's your sister-in-law?' Jo asked.

'Yes. They were married within a month of their first meeting and for the first few years of their marriage Denise accompanied him whenever she could. She enjoyed the excitement, the uncertainty of it all.' A fleeting coldness passed over his face before he shrugged it off. 'To give her her due, she helped Dave immensely every inch of the way,' he added expressionlessly.

'She went into all the trouble spots?' Jo repeated incredulously. 'But . . . but what about Sam?'

'Sam's arrival upset the apple cart somewhat,' Jake told her. 'I'm afraid Denise didn't care much for motherhood and as soon as she could she deposited Sam with her mother and rejoined Dave. The only reason Sam was with them in Central America was the fact that her grandmother had suffered a mild stroke and needed complete rest. The hotel where the news team were staying was hit by a shell and both Dave and Denise were killed, along with a dozen others. By some miracle Sam survived, but before the rescue squad could reach her she'd crawled through the debris to her mother's body. That's where they found her.' He sighed. 'Hence the nightmares.'

'Oh, Jake, how terrible,' Jo said softly, reaching across the table to cover his hand with hers. 'So you went over to bring her home?'

His hand moved, his fingers linking with hers, holding her firmly. 'Ordinarily Sam would have gone back to her grandmother who has virtually raised her, but the news of Denise's death brought on another stroke. She's now slowly recuperating with her other daughter in South Australia. So,' he expelled a breath, 'Sam's with me.'

'She . . . she thinks the world of you.' Jo's voice came out unevenly. She let her hand rest in his, not wanting to disturb the easy closeness that surrounded them.

'Mmm,' he murmured, the pad of his thumb beginning to brush the palm of her hand, and the entire timbre of the moment charged dramatically, charging the air with an electrified awareness.

That awareness caught Jo like a blow to the solar plexus and she tried to pull her hand from his hold on her. His fingers tightened, his eyes arrogantly daring her to break away from his gaze. They sat like that, unmoving, for immeasurable seconds before Jo expelled the breath that had been caught within her.

'I . . . It's late. I think I'll go back to bed.' She pushed back her chair, her hand still trying to free itself. 'Although there's not much left of the night.'

Jake stood up with her, his eyes going down to their locked hands before he slowly released her fingers. 'No, there isn't,' he said huskily, and the hair on Jo's scalp prickled as she turned and walked out of the kitchen, her heightened senses honed to his every movement.

Her over-sensitised hearing recorded every breath he took, every footstep, as he followed her back along the hallway past Sam's room where the child lay fast asleep. At last Jo reached her own room and pushing the door back she stepped inside, turning back to bid Jake goodnight in the most casual voice she could muster.

He had paused by her door, his eyes leaving her face to fall down over the rise of her breasts to the swell of her hips and the bare golden tan of her legs, and her heart faltered momentarily but he continued past her.

'Don't you mean good morning?' he muttered harshly, and as Jo stood transfixed he stopped again, turning around to face her, body weight balanced on one hand resting flat against the wall. 'You know, that's what I'd like to say to you in the mornings, Jo, when I wake up beside you.' His voice reached out huskily to caress her, his eyes glowing embers rendering her immobile. 'And goodnight the moment before we fall asleep.' He pushed away from the wall, changing in that split second from indolent seducer to stalking predator. 'Yes, walking away from you tonight is well nigh an impossibility for me right now,' he said self-derisively, and came towards her.

CHAPTER EIGHT

FOR one split second Jo stood suspended in disbelief,
her hand clutching the half opened door, and then she
darted into her room, almost throwing the door closed
behind her. But her moment of hesitation had cost her
dearly and Jake was far too fast for her. Even with her
weight against the door he had little trouble forcing
her backwards so that he could step inside her bedroom.

His strong bare arms imprisoned her, one on either
side of her body, and she turned to face him, flattening
herself against the door. They stayed like that, unmoving, facing each other, only their eyes touching.

With every moment that passed Jo could feel herself
succumbing to the practised seduction that emanated
from every inch of his powerful body. Those dark blue
eyes, black coals in the semi-darkness, roved over her
face, her straight nose, high well-formed cheekbones,
the smooth line of her jaw, and settling for breathtaking
moments on the tremble of her mouth. Jo's lips
opened, her tongue-tip moistening their sudden dryness, and Jake's body grew even more tense as his eyes
seemed to trace the outline of her mouth before his
gaze slid down over the column of her throat to settle
on the agitated rise of her breasts.

Jake sighed raggedly. 'Do you realise just how much
I want you, Jo?' he whispered thickly, and ran one
fingertip lightly along the line of her jaw, feather-soft
over the sensitive curve of her lips, down the line of
her throat to stop at the V-opening of her terry-towelling bathrobe that arrowed provocatively the valley
between her breasts.

She knew she should escape from him, make some attempt to break from his spell, but her body burned, ignited by the fire in his eyes which rendered her immobile, deaf to all but the sounds of each breath he took, blind to all but the outline of his tall muscular body. Could this be a dream, an hallucination of her eager imagination? But surely this racing response throughout her entire body was real, the fluttering pulse at the base of her throat still tingling from the touch of his finger, the hungering ache deep inside.

His finger left her body, but only so that his hand could claim the rise of one full breast. Jo's breathing literally stopped.

'No! Please, Jake, don't . . .' A jumble of words broke from her, propelled by the insistent demand for fulfilment his caress evoked and she went to push away his hand.

'Please, Jake, do,' he mimicked imperiously, and lowered his head towards her.

Jo turned her face away terrified, that her traitorous body would betray her if his sensual lips found hers. For the moment he contented himself with nibbling tantalisingly on her earlobe, running his lips down over her now vulnerable throat. Jo began to tremble anew, her knees feeling rubbery and ineffectual. When the tip of his tongue moved downwards following the line of her bathrobe she turned back to him.

'Jake, stop . . .'

Her words were lost in his mouth as his lips swooped to claim hers, moving slowly, sensuously encouraging, lifting her ever upwards. As his drugging kisses deepened his body drew closer with deliberate delay, until his whole solid length rested against her. The hardness of his thighs, the flatness of his stomach, the rock-ruggedness of his chest seered through the thinness of her robe, the flimsy gossamer of her nightdress. She smouldered with the awareness of every minute nuance of his body, every tension-filled tremor transmitting itself to her own ardour-thirsty body.

Jake's hand found and dispensed with the tie belt of her robe, slipping it over her shoulders where it fell to the floor. And then his hands returned to her breast. As her body responded to his caresses, completely powerless to offer any resistance, Jo moaned softly in her throat. Her arms reached around him, her fingers probing the furrow of his backbone.

'My robe,' he said huskily against her lips, 'untie it!'

Feeling for the belt, Jo's fingers shakily undid the knot, her hands slipping intimately over the smooth skin of his waist luxuriating over the sleekness of his taut torso, making a slowly physical exploration of his strong physique.

Pushing aside the thin strap of her nightdress, his lips trailed over her shoulder uncovering one full breast, a dome of alabaster in the faint moonlight, and his tongue tantalised her, destroying every last skerrick of her restraint.

With a groan he propelled her against him again, his lips taking desperate possession of hers in a kiss that reached down into her very soul. Jo's fingers crept downwards of their own volition over his naked body, exulting in his arousal, and her hands drew his hips against her with an urgency that matched his own.

At some time her nightdress fell to the floor to join her bathrobe, and Jake swung her into his arms and deposited her on the bed she had left some other century ago. Shrugging off his own robe, he lowered himself on to the single bed beside her, his hands running over the rounded contours of her body.

'My God, you're so beautiful,' he said heavily, his voice deep and ardent. 'Even more beautiful than I imagined you'd be.'

His lips found her breast again and Jo's fingers

twined into his hair, revelling in its dark thickness. Jake raised his head to look down at her, their faces illuminated in a shaft of moonlight beaming through a gap in the curtained window.

'I've wanted you this close to me for what seems like a lifetime,' he drew a ragged breath, 'a long barren lifetime,' he breathed. 'And I've never wanted a woman more than I've wanted you, Jo. Nor wanted to admit it,' he finished softly so that she had to strain to hear his words.

His lips met hers and the kiss was long and luring, carrying Jo away, her senses flowing with Jake on the tide he was creating, shooting the rapids of a sensuous fervour she had never before in her life dared to dream she would experience.

Never had Mike's lovemaking even hinted at this mindbending, rapturous route. Not once in their married life had ... The first flicker of faltering misgivings gripped her, part guilt, part fear of the depth of the unknown sea she was about to plunge into, gave her conscious mind the airplay for which it had been unacknowledgedly clamouring, warning her to take care, that accompanying this heady ecstasy, this soaring on another higher plane must be the journey back to earth, the return to the day-to-day normality when she would have to face herself, live with any consequences of her actions.

Consequences, the warning voice screamed at her. Dear God, what was she doing? Jo froze. What if she were to become pregnant? She wasn't taking any precautions and Jake probably ... Oh, no! Not a child! Not that! Never that. She would never have another child, couldn't bear to go through the joy, the wonder, the ... the desolate, mind-destroying agony of loss.

'No!' The word came out hoarsely in a voice she scarcely recognised as her own. 'No! No!' She moved her head back and forth, her hands flattening against his chest, pushing ineffectually against the rock-hard wall of muscle that was now not Jake but an adversary who could instigate all manner of untold pain and anguish.

Jake's body had stilled beside her, his hand motionless on her thigh where moments before it had been so potently arousing.

'No, Jake, I can't.' Tears oozed from beneath Jo's lashes as she saw his jaw tighten.

He bit off an imprecation. 'You can come this far and then decide you can't?' he rasped out through tight, controlled lips. His eyes bore down into her for countless seconds. 'You can't mean that,' he said at last in a tone bordering on threat, and his lips were crushing hers in a kiss that held no tenderness, was a pure punishment, cutting the softness of her inner lip, drawing blood.

With terror lending strength to her arms Jo fought him, beating against his shoulders and back. When his lips finally released hers he was breathing as heavily as she was and his eyes pierced into hers like cold black jets of steel. They stared at each other fighting to fill their lungs with air.

'For God's sake, why?' Jake ground out, his body still pinning hers to the bed.

Jo silently shook her head.

'Don't try to tell me it was all a show. I'm no inexperienced youth you can deceive with a play-act. You wanted me as much as I wanted you, didn't you?' he demanded.

When Jo remained silent, her face turned away from him, his fingers grasped her jaw, dragging her face none too gently to meet his eyes.

'Didn't you?' he repeated harshly, and Jo closed her eyes, making a feeble affirmative movement of her head. His fingers tightened painfully and then released her as he raggedly expelled the breath he had been holding.

'I suppose there's a reason,' he said sarcastically.

Jo made no comment as she was incapable of uttering a sound, her vocal cords locked in her throat, and his lips twisted cynically.

'Which you aren't going to disclose, it seems. Do enlighten me, Jo.' His tone chilled her to the bone.

How could she explain to him the tearing agony? In this moment of frustrated passion, that until her sanity had returned had promised them both such ecstatic fulfilment, how could she even begin to tell him about her failures, as a wife and ... About her beautiful Jamie and the guilt she had built piece by piece into a giant skyscraper about her until that night of the accident when it had cracked and fallen apart, breaking her in body and soul.

'Am I supposed to guess?' he quipped with cold humour. 'Well, let's see! It can't be that I don't turn you on, because we both know it's oh, so obvious that I did just that. And it can't be because you're bent on retaining your virginity, can it, *Mrs* Harrison?' He gave a mirthless laugh. 'Come on, Jo! You know what it's all about.'

Jo cringed away from him. 'Jake, please don't ... don't make it any worse,' she implored.

'Could it be any worse?' he ground out.

'Jake, I ... Mike ...' she swallowed painfully and began again. 'My husband ...'

He used a word she had never heard spoken in polite company and almost tore himself away from her to stand beside the bed. 'There's no need to say any more,' he said between clenched teeth as he reached for his robe and folded it about his moon-kissed nakedness, his still aroused maleness. 'I'm not about to play stand-in for a dead man,' he growled cruelly. 'I guess I don't want you as much as I thought I did.'

'Oh, Jake, I'm ...'

'For God's sake spare me any pitying apologies,' he cut in, 'because I'm so close to taking you and to hell with your consent for the basic animal motive that you're a woman, any woman, and I need a woman, that any tearful "I'm sorry's" could tip the scales against you.'

Without another glance he turned and left her, closing the door behind him with a restrained explosive click.

· Jo lay where he had left her, the warmth of the impression of his body turning chill, tingling across her skin. Her tears had dried and an arctic ache throbbed within her. A soft groan, half humourless laugh escaped her at the thought that he could imagine she still loved Mike, wanted to remain faithful to his memory.

Guilt clutched at her again. What had she said to place him under such a misapprehension? Perhaps it was for the best that he believed what he did, she tried valiantly to convince herself, and failed miserably.

She had never been more ashamed of herself than she was at this moment. How could she have allowed herself to lead Jake on so thoughtlessly? She felt the sting of her bruised lip and touched it gingerly with the tip of her tongue. He had been so angry. And Jo knew he had every right to that anger. She had behaved abominably, inexcusably. There was a sordid name for what she had done tonight.

Before she allowed herself second thoughts she sprang off the bed and retrieved her bathrobe, shivering at the brief reminder of Jake's hands slipping it from her shoulders. She opened the door, her bare feet carrying her silently along the hall way to Jake's room. Her steps faltered just a little as her fingers found the coldness of the doorknob but she forced herself to open the door and step into the room.

She would try to tell him about Jamie and about the

failure of her relationship with her husband. She couldn't let him go on thinking she was still in love with Mike. It couldn't be farther from the truth. And wasn't fair on Jake or on herself.

Her eyes were accustomed to the semi-darkness and she could see that his bed was empty. As she stood indecisively by the door a breeze stirred the floor-length curtains and she crossed to the sliding glass door which stood open. Stepping out on to the patio, she was in time to see Jake's figure disappearing down the steps that led to the beach.

'Jake!' The breeze caught her voice and tossed it mockingly back to her as Jake moved out of sight.

Jo could only return to her room, and once back in her bed the tears that threatened to choke her began to fall and she turned her face into her pillow, unable to curb their flow. There could be no denial that her actions tonight had irrevocably alienated Jake.

An excruciating pain twisted within her, breaking open the protective shell encasing her heart, a void buried deeply what seemed like eons ago. As some of the pain subsided she knew with earth-shattering clarity that her heart had gone. Jake Marshall had stolen it as surely as she was lying here hurting, as though his hand that had caressed her had reached deep down inside her and taken her heart from her body and now held it unsolicited in his keeping to bend or break it at his will.

Not until the first glow began to herald the impending sunrise did Jo finally fall into a light slumber. With the emotion-charged events of her broken night it was no wonder that she overslept.

A gentle touch on her arm roused her from sleep and she struggled to open her heavy languid eyelids. Her eyes flinched away from the bright sunlight streaming through the window and she groaned slightly in protest, her eyes feeling raw and gritty.

'You're a sleepyhead this morning, Jo,' teased Sam, climbing up on to the bed beside Jo and smiling down at her. 'Uncle Jake's almost finished making our breakfast. Aren't you going to get up ever today?'

Jake. The whole sordid mess came screeching back to her and she cringed at the thought of facing him again. And to attempt an apology would only add to her embarrassment.

The little girl was watching her expectantly and Jo dragged herself into a sitting position. 'I suppose I must.'

'Uncle Jake said five minutes to breakfast,' Sam scrambled from the bed. 'And,' she lowered her voice conspiratorially, 'I think you'd better come quickly, Jo, 'cause Uncle Jake looks very frowny.' She wrinkled up her forehead in imitation of her uncle.

'All right. Off you go and I'll be as quick as I can.' Jo threw back the bedclothes, her heart sinking. There was no prize for guessing the reason for Jake's ill-humour.

It didn't take her long to throw on a pair of faded jeans and a top, and she grimaced wryly to herself as she inadvertently chose a tailored shirt with a high demure neckline. Who was she trying to kid? Her fingers found the clasp at the top of her shirt, playing nervously with the button as she gingerly made her way to the kitchen. Jake had his back to her when she entered and she was certain she felt him tense when Sam spoke to her.

'We're having scrambled eggs on toast, Jo.' The little girl had already begun on her plate of fluffy golden eggs.

Jake turned around then, his eyes meeting Jo's for one chilling moment before he set her plate on the table and moved back to see to his own breakfast.

'I'm sorry I overslept,' Jo began as Jake took his

place opposite her, so close and yet so far away. 'I . . . thank you for making breakfast.'

'No worries,' he said noncommittally, and only Sam's chatter broke the ensuing silence of the adults.

From beneath her downcast lashes Jo stole a look at Jake scarcely believing their intimacy those few short hours ago. Had she really run her fingers through his thick dark hair? Smoothed her fingertips over the few strands that were peppered attractively with grey on either side of his head? Had she run her lips along that firm straight jawline, now set and uncompromising? And had she not exalted in the scorching possession of his lips? Her tongue found the sensitive bruising where his teeth had cut her lip and she winced slightly. Then her eyes settled on his hands and felt them moving over her once again, more potently devastating than any experience she had ever known before.

'Don't you like your scrambled eggs, Jo?' asked Sam innocently, and Jo came back to earth with a thud.

'Oh, yes, of course. I don't think I'm quite awake yet.'

Sam sighed loudly. 'I guess that's my fault, isn't it? I'm sorry I woke you up,' she said contritely, 'but I was afraid.'

It had crossed Jo's mind that the child hadn't remembered her broken night, and she smiled sympathetically. 'That's all right. Nightmares are frightening, aren't they?'

Sam nodded. 'I hate them,' she said flatly, and sighed again. 'Can we go down to the beach after breakfast?'

'Sure,' Jo smiled.

Jake placed his knife and fork on his empty plate with a restrained clatter and stood up. 'Well, I'll leave you to it, if you'll excuse me. I'll be in my study,' he said, and with barely a glance at Jo he left them.

'I think Uncle Jake's tired again,' remarked Sam understandingly.

Sam and Jo were enjoying a light lunch after their morning on the beach when Jake reappeared. He was wearing a navy scrub denim safari suit with a complementary pale blue and white striped shirt, and he looked so compellingly attractive that Jo was rendered completely breathless.

'I'm going up to the city,' he said, addressing the wall to the side of Jo's head. 'I expect I'll stay overnight and be back some time tomorrow.'

Jo's eyes fell to the table.

'Are you going to see Chrissie, Uncle Jake?' enquired Sam. 'Can Jo and I come too?'

'No, I don't think so, Sam. Not this time. I'll phone and ask Chrissie how she's coming along.' He shoved his hands in his pockets and absently jangled his car keys. 'Well, I'll be off. See you both tomorrow.'

Sam ran across to her uncle and he caught her, swinging her up into his arms and carrying her out on to the verandah with him. Jo followed a little more slowly.

' 'Bye, Uncle Jake. See you tomorrow.' Sam hugged Jake and planted a wet kiss on his cheek.

A lump developed painfully in Jo's throat and for one emotive moment she wished wholeheartedly that she could follow Sam, run across into his arms and bid him an equally spontaneous farewell.

The house seemed hollow and empty without Jake, even though had he been there he would most probably have kept to his study, and Jo ached for his return, suffering over finding some way to apologise, to explain her actions of the night before, but uneasily unwilling to revive it all again.

She retired to bed as soon as she had settled Sam down for the night, and although she fully expected to toss torturedly sleepless, her previous night's tumult took its toll and she was asleep as soon as her head touched her pillow.

The flash of car headlights on her window woke her with alarming suddenness without her being able to discern the reason for her awakening. However, the slamming of a car door brought her fully alert, her breath catching in her throat. She sat up, her ears straining for another sound.

Who could it be? Only Jake, surely? Then why didn't he come inside? It crossed her mind that they were completely isolated out here, any sound they made carried away on the sea breezes, and a moment's panic threatened to overcome her. Taking a steadying breath, she climbed out of bed and carefully opened her bedroom door. She would have to investigate. She wouldn't get any sleep if she didn't.

She moved quietly down the hallway and paused in front of the back door to listen for some reassuring sound, some indication that the late-night caller was Jake. A thud, as though someone had tripped on the steps, had her heart in her mouth and when it was followed by a muffled oath in a familiar deep voice Jo's legs almost gave way with relief.

Switching on the light, she unlocked the door and swung it open. Jake had his key poised ready to insert in the lock and her first sight of him gave her the impression that he was a little drunk. He had his suit jacket slung over his shoulder and his shirt was unbuttoned almost to the waist, looking as though it had been shoved irritatedly and none too tidily back into the waistband of his pants.

'Well, well, a welcome home committee,' he said sarcastically, and moved forward, his tread decisive and unhurried, belying his dishevelled appearance.

Jo stepped aside and slowly closed and relocked the door after he had entered the house. He threw his coat unceremoniously over a chair and walked into the kit-

chen, flicking on the lights as he went. Uncertainly Jo
followed him, standing in the doorway watching him
as he filled the electric kettle.

'Can I . . . shall I do that?' she asked haltingly.

He turned an enigmatic look on her. 'Do what?' he
asked suggestively, his eyes black and liquid.

'Make your tea.' Two bright spots of colour rose
over Jo's cheeks and she clasped her hands together,
not rising to his baiting.

'Don't bother,' he replied flatly, setting out a single
mug.

'I didn't expect you back tonight. You gave me quite
a fright. Did you . . . have a good trip?' Jo babbled,
her commonsense telling her to leave him be.

'Fine,' he said unencouragingly.

She swallowed. 'Well, I'll . . . goodnight.'

His muscular shoulders tensed. 'Do you want a cup?'
he asked almost graciously.

'I don't think so. Unless you want me to . . .' Jo's
voice died away.

'Good grief, woman!' he barked at her as he swung
back to face her. 'I'm quite capable of having a cup of
tea on my own!'

Jo's eyes fell, tears threatening to fall at his harsh
tone. 'I'm sorry. Goodnight.'

Jake bit off an exasperated exclamation. 'Jo?'

His tone had lost a lot of its aggression and she
stopped in the act of hurriedly returning to her room,
looking apprehensively back at him.

'I suppose I should apologise,' he said quietly, 'I'm
afraid I'm not in the best of humours.'

'That's all right.' His softened attitude brought more
tears to Jo's eyes. 'You must be tired.'

'Tired?' His mouth twisted and he gave a mirthless
laugh. 'Not tired enough, apparently.' His eyes flamed
over her. 'I only wish to God I were,' he muttered
self-derisively, and Jo took a step backwards.

Jake swore again and turned away from her. 'Go to bed!' he said curtly. 'And Jo,' her footsteps faltered although she didn't turn around, 'if I were you I'd lock my door,' he finished restrainedly.

Jo fled and her trembling fingers turned the key in her bedroom door as the tears coursed down her cheeks.

If she had thought there was a certain amount of tension between herself and Jake before then the next few days seemed even more taut and strained. Jake kept religiously to his study, although they rarely heard his typewriter. To Jo's super-sensitive nervous system his antipathy appeared to follow her about the house, suspending itself about her like a pall of inflammatory smoke.

Sleep eluded her with dogged regularity. She tried to read herself into tiredness, forcing herself to concentrate on the printed words, not allowing her thoughts to veer off at a tangent to Jake's nearness. As far as her physical tiredness went she succeeded, but her mind refused to submit to the relaxed oblivion of sleep.

She tried to escape by getting right away from the house, driving herself and Sam into the village to collect the groceries, staying long enough to browse through the shops, something she had never previously done. So shy of being recognised, she had always rushed into the supermarket and out again as fast as she could. Even going so far as buying herself and the little girl new dresses failed to drag her out of her emotional depression, and she began to panic inside, terrified of slipping back into her nervous state of a few short months earlier.

If only Maggie were here to talk to! Maybe she should go up to town. Maggie would put her into perspective again. And she could take Sam with her. To have Maggie's two little daughters to play with for a few days would also do Sam the world of good. But how could she explain Jake to her stepsister? She would have to admit to herself that she had fallen in love, fallen so hard that everything that had gone before had faded into a hazy yesterworld as though it belonged to some other Joelle Brent in some other life. And to concede that she was in love with Jake Marshall was a step she refused to take. It was as though she stood in a fog, not knowing if her next step would have her on solid ground or whirling in an empty, bottomless void.

But just to see Maggie again, to talk to her. She would ask Jake tonight at dinner, as the evening meal was the only time Jake joined them, if he had any objections to her taking Sam on a visit to Maggie's. She realised asking his permission in front of the child was an underhand way of going about it, but she knew she desperately wanted to get away. And if the truth be known Jake would welcome her removal from his proximity. However, all her psyching up turned out to be in vain, because Jake didn't appear at dinner, sending a message with Sam that Jo was to leave his meal in the oven for him to reheat later.

After Sam was asleep Jo wandered un-enthusiastically to her room, showered and changed into her nightgown and settled on her bed propped up with pillows trying to read. She persevered for half an hour, but the story couldn't hold her disquietened interest.

Maybe a little television? She rarely watched TV these days, but perhaps a variety show or a movie might hold her attention, calm her over-stimulated mind. The sound of Jake's typewriter came faintly into the living room as she switched on the television set and settled into an easy chair. Using the remote control unit, she flicked through the channels, deciding on a Britain-made comedy with which she was familiar and sat determinedly back to watch it. When the show came to an end half an hour later she felt much better.

The programme following it was a political debate, and not feeling in the mood for that after the comedy, Jo changed the channel again. Her hand froze as the oh, so very familiar face on the screen smiled out at her in living colour.

The hair-style was a little more severe, in keeping with the character being portrayed. The lips smiled, ruby red, their shape perfect. And blue eyes, fringed by dark lashes, glistened candidly at the camera. No clouds dimmed this beautiful girl's horizon, no burden sat heavily on those tanned shoulders. What was that old saying? The world her oyster. Well, to all outward appearances, the world was most definitely this beautiful girl's oyster.

Jo started to shake. It began as a slight tremor and soon she had to wrap her arms about herself to try to curb her trembling. Her face was colourless, as though she had seen a ghost. And in actual fact that was about what she had seen—a complete, a perfect ghost. It was the face she saw in the mirror each morning. Apart from one minor detail—major detail, she tortured herself cruelly. For the Joelle Brent on the screen had a smooth flawless face, unravaged by the jagged scar that the Joelle Brent of today carried with her like a brand.

With shaking hands Jo switched off the television set, watching with mixed feelings as that face faded from the screen. And she stared at that lifeless screen while the tide of jumbled memories flowed to play on her mind. Don't think! Don't think! she screamed at herself as she almost ran along the hall to her room, seeking a sanctuary, thinking the closing of her bedroom door could shut it all out of her mind.

Of course, it wasn't that simple. She paced up and down her room, yearning for the oblivion of sleep but fearing its dreadful consequences now that the past had been kicked up like a cloud of dust by the heels of a passing coincidence.

Jo had only ever had parts in three movies, doing most of her work live on the stage, and that movie tonight had been her first. It had led to a better part in the second one and an even bigger part in the third, which she had made just after her marriage to Mike. She knew her performance in her last movie had done much to help Mike secure her the female lead in a forthcoming movie which was to have the largest budget of any movie made in Australia. The break of the century, Mike had called it, and he had never forgiven her for not wanting to take the part.

Like a fight-worn animal Jo crawled into bed, drawing herself into a protective ball to lick her wounds. But her wounds had been buried too deeply for any salve to reach them.

How naïve and foolish she'd been way back then! So many memories, inconsequential and insignificant, returned to her of that day, a myriad impressions she hadn't even suspected she was storing away. Bright sunshine after a week of dismal showers. Buildings and gardens, trees and streets cleansed by the rain glistening like new. So much positive around her that it seemed impossible for there to be one single negative.

Until that afternoon when the doctor had confirmed her pregnancy she hadn't thought about having a family, at least not the way Maggie had. Suddenly knowing she had a child growing within her changed her entire outlook. She remembered the feeling of warmth that spread over her as she drove home, hugging her secret to her. Maggie was right: it was an indescribably beautiful experience.

That night she had prepared a special dinner for them, with candles and soft music, and she was in a fever of excitement by the time she heard Mike's key in the lock. Before he could shrug off his jacket she was in his arms and Mike swung her around, carrying her into the small living-room-cum-dining room.

'Hey, what's all this? What are we celebrating?' laughed Mike. 'You don't mean to tell me Aaron rang you before I could make it home?'

'No, Aaron hasn't phoned. Why?' Jo smiled enquiringly.

'Tell you later. So what are we celebrating?'

'Well, for a start, we've been married six months,' Jo teased.

'Is that all? I've got a better reason for us to celebrate than that.' Mike set her down.

'I did say it was only a start.' Jo glowed with happiness.

'Okay. What else?'

'I think I'll save mine. You tell me your reason first.'

'Oh, I suppose it's pretty tame really.' Mike put on an assumed, bored expression. 'I had quite a day, though. Aaron and I spent most of the afternoon with Bill Davies. We were discussing his next movie.' He paused. 'We decided you'd be perfect for the female lead.'

'The lead in one of Bill Davies' productions?' Jo repeated incredulously.

Mike nodded and beamed. 'This calls for that bottle of champers we've been saving.'

'Oh, Mike, I don't think I'll be able to do it.'

'Do what? The movie? Rubbish! They start filming in six months' time, just when the play ends. Fits in beautifully.' Mike waved her interruptions aside.

'It's not that, Mike. That's my news. I won't be the right shape for the part,' Jo laughed. 'I'm pregnant. Isn't that wonderful?'

Mike had stood open-mouthed before he sank down on to the nearest chair.

'Mike? What's the matter?' Jo's smile faded.

He just looked at her and she crossed the room

kneeling down in front of him. 'Mike, aren't you . . .? There'll be other parts,' she said softly, a chill gripping her heart.

'Don't be a fool, Jo,' he barked, and threw himself out of the chair and away from her, crossing to the bar to pour himself a large whisky. 'You know you need exposure or you'll be forgotten in this industry.'

Jo got to her feet and shook her head. 'I think I have more faith in my talent than that, Mike.' She turned away from him. 'Anyway, it's too late now.'

He finished his drink and came over to turn her back to face him. 'Jo, I'm sorry. You took me by surprise, that's all. You know we decided no family for a couple of years at least.'

Jo nodded. 'I didn't get pregnant on purpose, Mike,' she said evenly.

'I know, I know.' His hands rubbed her shoulders. 'It'll be all right. We can have other children later.'

'Other children?' she whispered. 'What do you mean?'

'I mean we can . . . well, it's a safe and simple operation these days.' His eyes didn't meet hers.

'You mean have an abortion?'

'Jo,' his hands tightened on her shoulders, 'the time's not right to have a family now. There's your career . . .'

'And yours,' Jo said bitterly.

'Yes, damn it, and mine!'

'And without my career yours won't move,' Jo said instinctively.

'Not as quickly as I want it to.'

'Is that why you married me, Mike?' she asked quietly.

'Don't be ridiculous! You know why I married you,' he turned away from her to lean his hands on the windowsill. 'Jo, I have to be honest with you. I'm just not ready for the dirty nappy, walking-the-floor domestic bit. I don't think we should have the baby.'

'I'm not murdering my child,' Jo said flatly.

Without a word Mike left the flat. From that
moment on they had never discussed the child, and
from that moment their marriage ceased to exist. They
were two strangers living in the same four walls. To
please Mike Jo went back to work two weeks after
Jamie was born.

Jo dashed the tears from her face. Mike had been
right: she should have had an abortion. Then there
would have been none of the agony afterwards when
... Don't think! Don't think! She squeezed her eyes
tightly closed, blanking out the heartrending flashback,
painting her mind with the protective coating of dull
grey nothingness.

At some stage she must have fallen asleep, for the
greyness was peeled away and she tumbled into the
terror again—the rend of sheering steel, the cold damp
blackness, the pain. And then the awful numbness that
was horrifically no respite at all.

No. No more. Jo cried out in her sleep, her hands
groping for reassurance, scratching for a handhold to
drag herself back out of the recurring dream. And for
the first time she wasn't clutching at nothingness.
Strong arms clasped her, gathering her against a warm
and solid safety.

'Jo, it's all right—I'm here. You're safe,' a deep voice
murmured soothingly.

'Jake?' Jo was almost awake now, recognised his
familiar voice, peered into the semi-darkness at the
shape of his dark head.

'Mmm.' He guided her head against his shoulder,
his hand gently soothing her hair.

'Oh, Jake. Poor Jamie . . .' Jo took a shuddering
breath and squirmed closer into his arms. 'Jake, hold
me.' She felt the nakedness of his leg against hers and
somewhere in the back of her mind she realised he had

slid his body into bed beside her. A quiver of warning passed over her even as her senses responded to move her body into the hard lines of his, moulding herself to his length as though they were made especially for each other. This was madness—but such a heavenly madness. She sighed languidly.

'Jake, you should go now,' she murmured sleepily, not attempting to put an inch of space between their bodies.

'I know,' he said, touching his lips softly to her temple. 'Just relax and go back to sleep.'

'But . . .' she moved slightly.

'Jo,' he said warningly. 'Keep still and I may be able to console myself with half a cake tonight. If I remain sane, that is,' he finished on a soft groan.

Jo smiled, settling contentedly against him, inhaling the clean male odour of him, and exhaled happily, her sigh fanning his neck. She heard him catch his breath and his arms tightened about her momentarily before he forced them to slacken and Jo slid into a peaceful slumber, shielded by Jake's strength, all the terror behind her.

CHAPTER NINE

Moving her cramped muscles, Jo slowly drifted awake, blinking into the blackness. She yawned faintly, wondering what could have woken her up. Not the sun streaming through the window, that was for sure, because the sky was just beginning to lighten preparing itself for dawn. Her arm felt quite numb and she shifted it carefully, freezing as it came into contact with a smooth living solidness.

Her eyes strained into the darkness, her whole body stiff as the fact fully registered that Jake was stretched out beside her. Now it was flooding back to her—the movie, the dream. She shuddered. The cold blind terror. And then there was Jake's arms holding her fast, safe against his warm body.

Jo swallowed convulsively, some of her stress leaving her, and she couldn't stop herself returning to the absolute safety of that closeness. The rhythmical rise and fall of Jake's chest indicated that he still slept, and secure in this knowledge, she gave her impulses free rein, luxuriating in the sensuality of allowing her body to mould itself to his. She felt herself blush when she realised he was completely naked, and her heartbeats began to drum in her ears.

Turning her head, she rested her lips against his bare shoulder, moving the tip of her tongue over his tanned skin, the taste of him an ambrosial nectar, and she closed her eyes as a flood of tumultuous feeling washed over her.

'Oh, Jake! If only . . .' she whispered to herself, the words catching in her throat as a hundred silent pleas sprang into her mind.

Jake stirred and turned towards her, his arm going out to encircle her, pulling her against him. His lips found hers in the darkness, moving gently with sleepy sensuousness.

'If only what?' he asked softly before his lips nuzzled her earlobe, sending lightning flashes of desire from one end of her body to the other.

'You're awake?' she mumbled inconsequentially.

'Mmm, I hope so,' his voice rumbled, deeply vibrant. 'If I'm not don't wake me,' he groaned, and his lips returned to her mouth with a desperate demand.

Jo responded spontaneously, answering his insistence with a fervour that set her senses spinning. When Jake's hands began to caress her through the thinness of her nightdress she arched against him and murmured his name into the curve of his throat. Her hands eagerly helped him as he lifted the material over her head, his breath catching as the first tinge of dawn highlighted the full mound of her breast that throbbed for his touch.

Her fingers explored the curves and planes of his muscular form a tiny flicker expressing shock at her lack of constraint. The rightness of this mutual magnetism drove all thought of shyness from her, leaving her with no qualms about giving herself to Jake with all the love that her renascent heart held for him.

The muscles of his thigh tensed as her gently caressing hand moved downwards and his lips tantalised first one aroused nipple and then the other. As his body covered hers he huskily sighed her name, and to Jo the sweetness of that sound brought tears of happiness to her eyes. There was no thought of holding back, they had both progressed too far for that, and the only air in the universe was the air they breathed, the only sounds the music of their bodies' harmony, the only existence this shared moment of craving desire.

Their lovemaking created a new dimension for Jo.

Until now she had been lying unwittingly dormant, her inner self, her driving force untouched, poised, waiting for Jake to carry her aloft along a new and entranced pathway that she had never dared to dream existed.

Jake. She sighed his name as she floated fulfilled down from the exalted heights to which he had lifted her, a smile of pure wonder curving her still tingling lips. Jake. To think that such a short time ago she had never met him, and yet she felt she had known him all their lives and beyond.

When she woke up the sun was streaming in on her and the smile on her lips widened, only momentarily faltering when she turned her head to find that Jake had gone. But the indentation in the pillow from the pressure of his dark head remained, and Jo turned and wrapped her arms about that pillow, stretching her still naked limbs languorously. She loved Jake so much. And he . . .

A tiny cloud hovered on her rosy horizon. She knew exactly how she felt about Jake, she loved him passionately, but what were his feelings for her? Last night there had been no words spoken. He hadn't actually told her he loved her, while she . . . Oh God, ghad had che caid·

Jo'c gbii on dhe iillog dighdened and che cloced heb eiec. Ac che had fallen acleei che bemembebed meb-mebing hic name. Ghad if che had ibofecced heb lofe fob him in dhad momend, cecebe in dhe headi afdebmadh of co gondboec an ehiebience· And ceiiocing he didn'd feel dhe came gai aboed heb·

Bed he had made lofe do heb ac dhoegh ... No. A sob caught in her throat. He had said he wanted her. He had never mentioned love. A cold chill clutched at her as her euphoric mood crashed about her and she realised her hand had gone to the scar on her cheek, following the jagged furrow. In the short time that she had been here the importance of that scar had faded away. Now it assumed mammoth proportions again. How could she have forgotten?

Her throat tight, Jo climbed out of bed and glanced at her bedside clock, her eyes widening in surprise when she saw it was after eleven o'clock. The house was perfectly quiet and she gathered her clothes together and hurried to have a shower.

Sam's room was empty and Jake's study door stood wide open. In the kitchen a note was propped up against the teapot, written in Jake's strong scrawl, 'We're on the beach.'

Jo sat down at the kitchen table and rested her head on her hands. How would she face him after her shameless behaviour of the early morning? If he thought she was easy and lacking in morals how could she honestly blame him?

Sam's cheerful voice floated in through the back door and her running footsteps followed by Jake's firmer tread had Jo sitting bolt upright, her hands clutching the table top, a dull flushing suffusing her cheeks.

'Hi, Jo! We had a swim while you were waking up.' Sam pressed her damp salty body against Jo.

'Yes. I overslept again,' Jo said quickly, trying not to look at Jake, but his presence was like a magnet drawing her eyes, and her gaze slid across the floor and moved upwards over his lithe muscular body. Just the sight of his tanned frame stirred up sensual memories and her heartbeats fluctuated unevenly.

At last her eyes met his and she hurriedly looked back at the child, her heart sinking. He looked so remote, as though the night had never been, was just a figment of her heightened imagination, and Jo had to swallow the painful lump that rose in her throat.

'Uncle Jake said you were tired.' Sam planted a wet kiss on Jo's cheek and Jo hugged the child to her, needing to give some of the pent-up love she had stored up for Jake to someone who would accept it without question or reservation, and Sam grinned happily, hugging Jo back.

'Better have a shower and change, Sam.' Jake spoke at last.

'Okay, Uncle Jake.' Sam skipped past him and stopped, turning back to Jo. 'Will you come and help me decide which shorts and top to wear?' she asked, her head on one side.

'Of course.' Jo stood up, her heart racing as she approached Jake, her step faltering as he continued to block the doorway. Nervously, she raised her eyes.

'Jo,' he said softly, 'about last night . . .'

'Jo!' called Sam from her bedroom.

Jake's jaw tightened and he ran his hand through his damp hair. 'We'll talk later,' he said as he stepped out of the kitchen and disappeared towards his room.

Sam and Jo were busily digging in their vegetable garden after lunch when the sound of a car coming slowly down the driveway had them straightening curiously. Jo's hand went to the scarf covering her hair ensuring that it was in place and she pushed her sunglasses more firmly on her nose.

'It's a taxi,' said Sam as the orange Ford pulled into sight. 'Who could it be?'

The woman who stepped gracefully from the back seat of the taxi could be no one else but Lexie Vale, thought Jo, a second before Sam's small figure stepped so close to Jo's side that Jo had to steady herself. She looked down at the little girl and Sam's face had puckered into a worried frown.

'It's Lexie,' she whispered almost desperately, her hand finding Jo's.

A multitude of conflicting emotions rose up in Jo, threatening to choke her. Until this moment she hadn't given this woman a thought, and now Jake's fiancée stood before her and she was overcome with shame. How could she have forgotten that Jake was not free, was morally bound, his love promised to this coldly beautiful creature?

Suddenly their lovemaking took on a shadow of sordidness and the nausea clutched at Jo's stomach. What sort of woman was she? Jo asked of herself.

And Jake. What excuse could he have for forgetting that he was engaged to one woman while he betrayed her with another? And she'd thought that he was . . . That he was what? An honourable man? That was almost funny. If Jake was dishonourable then what adjective could she apply to herself? There was a time when she would have staked her life on her own integrity.

Lexie paid off the taxi driver and directed him to leave her suitcase on the verandah. Taking a deep breath, Jo set down her spade and stepped forward with Sam still clinging closer than her shadow.

'Can I help you?' Jo called, and the other girl stopped as she was about to walk up the steps and turned back to face Jo.

The perfectly made-up green eyes narrowed as they followed Jo's approach, moving almost insolently from the top of Jo's scarf wrapped head to the tips of her sandal-clad feet. Jo wished she could have had the moral support of more respectable attire. Her faded denim shorts and stretched and misshapen T-shirt were no match for the other girl's exclusive outfit.

Lexie's green two-piece suit was the precise shade of the green of her eyes and the russet swirls in her green blouse were the exact colour of her short close-cropped hair. Every curve and line spoke of expense and sophistication.

'Help me? No, I don't think so.' The husky voice was just a little higher than it had sounded on the telephone. 'I'm here to see Jake.'

Jo slipped off her gardening gloves and left them in the wheelbarrow as she walked towards the other girl. 'I'll tell him you're here.'

'Don't bother, Mrs Harrison.' Lexie's whole stance was arrogance. 'It is Mrs Harrison, isn't it?'

'Yes, that's right.' Jo stopped, her own guilt making it an effort for her to meet the other girl's eyes.

'Yes.' The red lips thinned. 'Well, just carry on doing what you're doing.' She flapped her hand in the direction of the garden. 'I have been here before, so I'm quite capable of finding Jake for myself.' She turned dismissingly on her high-heeled shoes and walked up the steps.

'She didn't even say hello to me,' said Sam softly. 'If Uncle Jake had been here she'd have hugged me and kissed me.' She wrinkled her small nose distastefully. 'Why do you suppose she's here, Jo?'

'I don't know.' Jo's eyes rested on the doorway through which the other girl had disappeared. 'To see your uncle,' she added flatly. Or . . . she flinched at the thought. Perhaps Jake had realised he's made a mistake this morning and asked Lexie to come down to remind himself that he was already committed. Jo's heart throbbed painfully. The most sensible thing for her to do was to leave them to it. If Jake's fiancée was here she could care for Sam and Jo would be free to go. And that was most probably what he had in mind, she thought, feeling the familiar numbness begin to take hold of her body again.

'But, darling,' Lexie's long scarlet-tipped fingers, settled on Jake's arm, sharply white against Jake's sun-tan, 'I thought we could make a night of it—have dinner and catch a show, play the pokies, dance.' Her voice ended on a husky familiar note.

'We can't take Sam to the R.S.L. Club,' Jake replied. 'We'll go to a family restaurant.'

'Oh, Jake!' Lexie pouted. 'That doesn't sound like you. What's happened to you, vegetating down here in the country? Where's all your staying power? You used to be able to dance all night,' she purred. 'Don't tell me you're getting old?' Her laughter tinkled brittly, abrading Jo's nerves.

'Maybe I am at that,' Jake smiled back.

'And besides,' Lexie moved closer to Jake's side, her eyes gazing up at him, 'Sam may prefer to stay at home with Mrs Harrison.'

Jake's eyes went to Jo and she swallowed painfully, her mouth dry as she wished fervently that she could be any place but here watching this woman display her proprietorial hold on Jake, knowing achingly that Lexie had every right to expect Jake's allegiance.

'I'm not going if Jo's not going,' said Sam, eyeing Lexie unhappily.

'There you are,' said Lexie, undaunted by Sam's reluctance for her company.

'Jo's coming, too,' said Jake firmly, untangling himself from Lexie's arm. 'I'll ring for a reservation.'

'Great!' Sam clapped her hands. 'And Jo and I can wear our new dresses. Wait till you see them, Uncle Jake, they're really pretty.'

Jake smiled down at his niece. 'I'm sure they will be.' His eyes slid up to meet Jo's before he gave his attention back to Sam. 'And that doesn't mean you can take all afternoon to get dressed.' He ruffled Sam's hair. 'One hour on the dot we leave, ready or not.'

Sam giggled. 'Come on, Jo,' she took hold of Jo's hand. 'We'd better get started right away. Do you think I should have my hair in pigtails or just leave it combed out?'

There was nothing left for Jo to do but to follow Sam out of the room, but she shivered as she left, feeling Lexie's cold green eyes boring into her back, admitting guiltily that she could sympathise with the other girl's understandable displeasure.

And that Lexie Vale was not pleased with Jo's presence in the Marshall household was a fact she had made patently obvious from the moment she arrived. What had transpired between Jake and his fiancée, Jo didn't know, didn't care to think about, but she had managed to keep both herself and Sam out of their way all afternoon by taking the little girl on to the beach.

If Jake had any remorse for his actions he was covering up very well, his face closed and inscrutable whenever Jo encountered him. How she wished she knew the secret of turning herself on and off for the moment, the way he seemed to have done.

Gently sliding her new dress over her shoulders, Jo paused, gazing pensively at her reflection. Why was Jake insisting that she be included in their dinner outing? She wanted to go as little as Lexie wanted her with them. One would surmise that Jake would want his fiancée to himself ... So why take Sam and Jo along on what Lexie implied should be an intimate dinner for two? There seemed no reason for Jake's action.

Jo's eyes fell over her figure, only part of her taking in the unconscious allure of the feminine dress, the pale blue colour complementing her clear turquoise eyes and fair hair, the soft cotton knit material moulding her full breasts, narrow waist and nicely rounded hips. A touch of pale pink lip gloss completed her light make-up and she reached for her brush, gently smoothing the soft waves of her hair as it sprang back to curl softly to her shoulders. The hair-style she had cultivated since the accident fell close to her eye and over her cheek, effectively hiding the jagged scar. She tentatively patted the hair into place. As long as she kept out of the wind no one would even guess that the disfigurement was there.

She had even forgotten it was there herself these past

few days, she thought wryly, her lips twisting into a bitter little smile. She should have known better than to allow herself to fall under the spell of this household. The web had been woven by firstly the child and then by the potent attractions of Jake himself. Jo realised her knuckles were white where she clutched her brush and she gradually forced herself to relax and set the brush back on her dressing table.

Leaving her room with a wary reluctance Jo peeped into Sam's room to find it empty and continued on into the living room in search of the little girl. To her horror only Jake occupied the room, standing with his back to her, gazing out through the plate glass window at the seascape, his shoulders slightly hunched, almost dejected.

He was the very last person Jo wanted to find herself alone with, and she stood poised just inside the doorway. Perhaps she could leave quietly before he was aware of her presence, but even as the thought crossed her mind he turned from his silent contemplation of the sea, and in that unguarded moment Jo saw a certain bleakness in the blue intensity of his eyes.

'I didn't know you . . . I was looking for Sam,' she finished lamely, her cheeks hot.

'She's out the back on the verandah waiting impatiently to leave,' he said flatly.

'Oh. Well, I'll just go and . . .'

'Jo!' His barely restrained exclamation halted her as she began to make her escape and the pulse in her throat fluttered nervously as he strode across the room to stand in front of her only a hand's width from her instantly tensed body. Jo's mind screamed at her to leave him standing there, but the weakness in her limbs refused to make a move to follow her direction.

'Jo,' he repeated, deeper, huskier than before, this time his tone more asking than demanding, and a lump rose in Jo's throat. Her fingers clenched into fists in her effort to prevent herself from reaching out to touch him, to run her hands over the fine firmness of his chest, to feel the strong beating of his heart stirring beneath her caress.

The pain came then, a burning ache of wanting that completely robbed her of speech. She could only stand there looking at him, drinking in each facet of his handsomeness. His dark hair, lightly flecked with grey at the temples and still damp from his shower. The compelling blue-black of his eyes with their fringe of long dark lashes that should have been feminine but somehow only accentuated the exact opposite. The attractively chiselled planes of his face angling down to his firm jaw. And his lips. Lips whose line gave the precise impression of forcefulness and resolution that could so easily curve into an arousing sensuousness that lifted caressingly on to some higher plane.

Oh, Jake, Jo cried out inside herself, why wasn't our time right? Why couldn't we have met before Mike, before Lexie, and before Jamie?

Some of her distress must have been visible on her face, for his jaw tightened and his hands were reaching out for her when Lexie stepped into the living-room. Jo started guiltily, moving back from the magnetic circle of Jake's attraction, her face flushing as Lexie's eyes rested on her trembling lips. The tension in the air almost buzzed in Jo's ears and she knew by the slight narrowing of Lexie's green eyes that the other girl was not unaware of it.

'Ready, darling?' she asked silkily, moving over to Jake's side and taking his arm.

'I'll . . . I'll check that Sam's ready,' Jo stammered, and hastily left them, feeling as though the devil himself sat on her shoulders.

The three-quarters of an hour drive up to Tweed Heads seemed to last for an eternity to Jo, but she sat resignedly beside Sam in the back seat only half listening to the little girl's excited chatter. Lexie sat in the front beside Jake directing her conversation to him, pointedly excluding Jo as she discussed people and places that were only familiar to Jake. At least the people were not known to Jo, but the general circle, a round of social events that seemed, judging by her conversation, to occupy the majority of Lexie's time, had a remembered familiarity. After she had met Mike he had taken her to so many similar gatherings that she had lost count of them. She had to be seen, Mike had said, and acquaintances were always useful. Jo had always felt a fraud and afterwards when Mike had ceased to insist that she accompany him Jo had only experienced relief.

Somehow Jo wouldn't have thought that kind of scene would have interested a man like Jake Marshall. Her eyes moved over the back of his head, noticing the way his hair was shaped neatly to the collar of his crisp white body shirt. Yearning to reach out and touch him, Jo glanced across at Lexie, reluctantly admiring the way the other girl kept up a flow of bright chatter in the face of Jake's infrequent and unencouraging replies. Had Jake been as noncommittal with her Jo knew she would have lapsed into a strained and hurt silence.

Her eyes returned to Jake, her gaze locking with his in the isolation of the rear view mirror, and it was though an electric shock passed through her for those few seconds before he of necessity returned his eyes to the road. For the remainder of the journey Jo restricted herself to looking out of the side window, her mind not registering the passing scenery.

The meal in the popular restaurant was exceptionally good, although it crumbled in Jo's mouth like ashes and she was as jumpy and nervous as a kitten. Most of her agitation was due to Jake's nearness, the way her eyes met his across the small dining table each time she looked up from her plate. And his gaze didn't seem to leave her. Even when he leaned slightly sideways to catch something Lexie whispered his eyes remained on Jo, and the trembling in the pit of her stomach intensified until she could scarcely swallow a mouthful.

And apart from Jake's disturbing proximity this was by way of her first public appearance since the accident and the ordinary everyday sounds of the diners about her chattering, clinking cutlery, clattering crockery, seemed to echo inside her. What if someone recognised her? She cast a quick glance about the room, seeking a familiar face, and then chastised herself severely. Who could possibly recognise her? It was well over a year since the accident and people soon forgot, as Mike was fond of impressing on her.

'Tell me, Mrs Harrison,' Jo looked up to find Lexie's eyes resting calculatingly on her, 'have I met you somewhere before?'

'No.' Jo's heart almost stopped.

'Are you positive?' Lexie pressed.

'Yes. I'm . . . I'm sure I would have remembered,' Jo's voice faltered and her palms were cold and damp as she clutched her hands together under the table not allowing herself to look at Jake, hoping fervently that he wouldn't say anything about her past career.

'Mmm. Funny,' Lexie frowned, 'you look a little familiar to me now that you have your hair out. What did you do before you took up child minding?'

'N . . . Nothing. I haven't worked for some time.' Jo nervously took a sip of her wine.

'Can we have some ice cream, Uncle Jake? Or maybe some fruit salad?' Sam piped up, and Jo almost sighed thankfully.

'Sure. How about you, Lexie? Jo?' Jake asked. Both Jo and Lexie shook their heads.

'Well, suppose we go over to the dessert bar and choose something really delicious.' Jake stood up and helped Sam off her chair. 'Will you excuse us for a few minutes?' They walked off together hand in hand, leaving Jo and Lexie alone.

Slowly Lexie took a cigarette from her gold case, putting the cigarette between her red lips and lighting it with a matching lighter. 'And how long do you intend helping Jake out, Mrs Harrison?' she asked, exhaling a small cloud of smoke.

'Only until Chrissie is fit enough to return,' Jo replied.

'I see.' Lexie's eyes contemplated the glowing end of her cigarette and then moved to Jo.

Like a snake, Jo thought, eyes cold and measuring as a snake's, waiting for the moment to make a death strike.

'Chrissie's accident must have been quite a windfall for you.'

Jo looked directly at the other girl in disbelief. 'How can you say anyone's accident is a windfall?' she asked quietly.

'Oh, come now, Mrs Harrison,' Lexie waved her cigarette in an expressive arc, 'Jake's not here, so there's no need to keep up this pretence with me.'

'Pretence?' Jo repeated, her first thought being that Lexie had remembered where she had seen Jo previously. 'I really have no idea what you're talking about.'

Lexie's high laugh cut across Jo's words. 'I think you do. You've managed to insinuate yourself into a comfortable little niche in Jake's household, and I see you've been clever enough to get the child on your side.'

Jo took a deep steadying breath. 'I am simply filling in for Chrissie,' she said distinctly, wishing it was possible to stand up and leave the other girl sitting there. 'And I genuinely like Sam,' she added.

'Oh, I don't blame you,' Lexie said grandly. 'It must

have been quite a shock to be cast back into the work force, to have to fend for yourself after being widowed. You did say you were widowed?' she asked suggestively.

'Yes, I did. And if you're trying to say I'm looking for a meal ticket then you couldn't be more wrong. I'm quite financially independent.'

Lexie raised her wine glass to her lips and sipped the light Moselle. 'Lucky you,' she said, her eyes going to the liquid moving in her glass as she twisted the fine stem in her scarlet tipped fingers. Her eyes suddenly flashed up to Jo's face. 'Jake's a rather gorgeous animal, isn't he?' A cool smile lifted her lips. When Jo made no effort to reply, 'Well, Mrs Harrison? Isn't he a handsome devil?'

'I suppose he is rather good-looking.' Jo kept her voice even and detached, her eyes on the tablecloth.

'Rather!' Lexie drawled, her brittle laugh affecting Jo like the squeaking rasp of chalk on a blackboard. 'But just a friendly little word of warning, because I wouldn't like to see you get hurt.'

'Look, Miss Vale, I . . .' Jo began.

'Now, now!' Lexie patted Jo's hand where it rested on the table and Jo couldn't prevent herself from snatching her hand away. 'You're an attractive girl and so young to be widowed. How long ago did you lose your husband, by the way?'

'Over a year ago,' Jo replied quietly, willing Jake and Sam to hurry back to the table.

'There! You see you're just at a susceptible stage and so very vulnerable.' Lexie frowned sympathetically. 'But, believe me, it's an absolute waste of time setting your sights on Jake because—well, Jake and I . . .'

'All this is quite pointless, Miss Vale. I'm aware of your engagement to Jake,' Jo said flatly, 'so may we please change the subject?'

'Of course.' Lexie ran the tip of her finger around the edge of her wine glass. 'Tell me, did Jake himself tell you we were engaged?'

'Yes.' Jo looked away, hoping the other girl couldn't see the pain she felt reflected on her face.

'Oh, good. Well, I can see you're a sensible person, but you know, I felt I had to warn you. Poor Jake! He's too damn handsome for his own good. He always has hordes of women falling all over him, and I suppose he wouldn't be human if once or twice a pretty face didn't turn his head.'

Jo swallowed painfully as a knife-edge pierced her heart. The implication was that she was simply a pretty face that turned his head. Pretty face! Jo had to quell a burst of hysterical laughter that threatened to break from her.

'But,' Lexie shrugged, 'he always comes back to me, the arrogant swine, and I'm just too weak to refuse to forgive him,' she pouted. 'Personally, I don't think Jake has a terribly high opinion of most women since his first love ran off with his older brother.'

Jo's eyes widened and Lexie nodded.

'Hard to believe, isn't it? That was years ago, of course, but apparently Jake wasn't exciting enough for Denise, so she threw him over for Dave. I guess that's why he took on the responsibility of the child, even though I think she'd be far better off with Denise's family.'

Both Lexie and Jo sought out Jake's tall figure as he made his way back to the table with his niece.

'All I can say is, Dave Marshall must have been really something,' Lexie said softly.

Jo felt quite physically sick, wondering how she was going to make it through the remainder of the evening. Her eyes sought Jake's for some expression, some slight glimmer of reassurance that all this was just another dream, a torturing nightmare, and that she would eventually awaken to the sound of the sea breaking on the beach, to the sound of Sam's laughter, to the click of Jake's typewriter, to anything rather than this pain-filled ordeal of swapping confidences with this cold uncaring creature to whom Jake belonged.

Jake sat down laughing at something Sam said, and Jo felt part of her curl up and die. She had lived in the same house as he did. She had eaten meals with him. She had shared his bed for one brief wondrous night, knew the feel of his hard body, felt the throbbing of his racing heart beneath her fingers, and had fallen deeply and irrevocably in love with him. Only to find she scarcely knew him.

At some time during her soul-searching, sleepless night Jo decided finally she would have to get away, to make the break for her own self-preservation. To tell herself that she knew she shouldn't have moved over here gave her not one bit of solace, because against her own better judgment she had done just that.

How to manage her escape would be the problem. If it hadn't been for the child she would have gone, disappeared in the night, but with Jake planning to drive Lexie back to the city the next day she could hardly leave Sam to her own devices. But she had to get away. Jake would have to find someone else to care for his niece, because she couldn't afford to wait until Chrissie returned.

Throughout the next morning she tried to get a few moments alone with Jake to tell him of her decision, but each time she was foiled by either Sam's or Lexie's appearance nearby. After lunch Jake and Lexie set off together to drive up along the coast to visit friends of Lexie's leaving Jo with the knowledge that they would be returning later that evening and that Lexie's departure was postponed until the next day.

'I wish she was going home now,' Sam murmured as she stood on the verandah watching her uncle's car disappear up the driveway. 'She doesn't like me.'

Jo looked down at the little girl, putting an arm about her shoulders and thinking that Lexie was not overly fond of her either, and she sighed.

'Jo?' Sam gazed up at her. 'Do you think Uncle Jake might marry me when I grow up if I get to be as pretty as you are?'

Laughing reluctantly, Jo sat down on the step and lifted Sam on to her knee. 'You'll be beautiful and your uncle will spend all his time fending off lots of handsome young men who'll come calling.'

The little girl giggled, her blue eyes looking suddenly very much like Jake's, and Jo hugged Sam to her, wondering how she could ever have imagined the child was plain. Her heart ached. How was she going to bear leaving Sam behind, for she was now as much a part of Jo's life as her uncle was, and Jo had to blink back a flood of tears.

'I wish you'd stay with us until I'm grown up, Jo,' Sam said, her bottom lip trembling.

'Chrissie will be back soon,' Jo began her voice too bright.

'I know. But I'll miss you, Jo.' Sam's fingers played with the button on the top of Jo's shirt. 'And so will Uncle Jake. He likes you, too, I told you he does.'

That remained to be seen, Jo thought, her heart contracting painfully, but before she could make any comment a car came slowly down the driveway and Jo stood up apprehensively with Sam clutched in her arms. It could only be Jake. But why would he have returned so soon?

The car rounded the bend in the drive and drew to a halt, a tall thin figure unwinding himself from behind the steering wheel, and the bright sunlight caught the longish fair hair, turning it almost to white. Jo shielded her eyes with her hand and her mouth fell open in astonishment as she recognised the thin aesthetic features.

'Aaron!' she breathed hoarsely. 'What . . . How . . . how did you know where to find me?'

'Pure detection, my love,' he laughed a shade uncertainly, obviously unsure of his welcome. 'You should have known it was only a matter of time before I found you. How could I allow you to fade out of my life, you divine creature?' He struck a purely theatrical pose.

Jo swallowed. 'But I told Maggie not to . . .'

'Not to tell me where you'd gone,' he finished. 'And she didn't. You know Maggie, wild horses wouldn't have dragged it from her.'

'How, then?'

'I very underhandedly wangled a dinner invitation out of Maggie and Ben and while I was playing with the kids in the garden I got them talking about you, and out it came.' He grinned a little shamefacedly. 'I didn't get the exact address, of course, but I came down to stay with friends in Kingscliff and managed to ferret you out. There aren't many cottages along the coast here, so it was a process of elimination. I couldn't believe my luck when I drove in here and there you were.'

'Oh, Aaron!' Jo shook her head. Had he turned up just after her arrival at Maggie's cottage, before she'd met Sam and Jake, she would have run away from him in horror, because he was a link in the chain to the past. Now she could look at him with scarcely a twinge of pain for past memories, and she smiled slowly at him.

His grin widened and lit his hazel eyes. 'That's more like my old Jo,' he said softly, and they stood smiling at each other.

Sam wriggled in Jo's arms, her eyes on the stranger. 'Is he your boy-friend, Jo?' she asked quietly, her hands tightening around Jo's neck.

'Unfortunately not, poppet.' Aaron tickled Sam under the chin and she smiled shyly. 'Always wanted to be, but Jo wouldn't have me,' he said, an underlying sadness in his teasing words.

Jo's eyes fell away from his. Aaron had been a friend of Mike's and she knew how upset he had been when it became obvious that their marriage wasn't working out. The one time Aaron had tried to discuss it with Mike, Mike had pointedly told his friend to mind his own business. And Jamie had adored Aaron. Jo forced those memories away almost before she recalled them.

'Do you . . . would you like a cup of coffee?' Jo asked at last.

'Love one.' Aaron followed her inside. 'And what's your name?' he asked the little girl as Jo sat her down in the kitchen and turned to switch the kettle on to boil.

'Sam. Who are you?' Sam climbed on to a chair.

'I'm Aaron Daniel, and I used to work with Jo,' he replied, his eyes following Jo's movements.

Jo flushed at the look in his eyes and her hand went to her face, smoothing her scarf over her cheek.

'Maggie said, after much pumping, that you'd gone away to write,' he remarked as they sat at the table, and his eyes moved pointedly to the child.

'Yes. I guess I really came down here to——' she paused, 'rest. And to give Maggie and Ben a break from me,' she added lightly. 'Then Chrissie, the housekeeper here, broke her leg and I . . . I offered to look after Sam.'

Aaron nodded. 'You look great,' he told her, his eyes going to the concealing scarf, and Jo's hand fluttered upwards. 'More beautiful than before, Jo.'

'I think Jo's pretty, too,' piped up Sam, and both adults looked at her. 'And Jo says when I grow up I'll be pretty, too.'

'You know, I think Jo's perfectly right,' Aaron smiled at Sam, and she grinned back.

'Do you know my Uncle Jake?' she asked.

'No, I don't think I do.' He gave Jo a quick look.

'Oh.' Sam sighed. 'I've finished my milk, Jo. Can I go and play in my room?'

Jo nodded and when Sam left them she kept her eyes on the coffee mug in her hand.

'I meant it, Jo,' Aaron said softly.

'Meant what?' she looked up then, her eyes enquiring.

Aaron smiled crookedly. 'That I've yet to see a more photogenic face than yours.'

'Not any more, Aaron,' said Jo, and for the first time there was no bitterness, just a quiet acceptance, and she felt as though part of the heavy weight she carried was lifted from her. 'And, do you know, it doesn't really matter to me any more.' She drew off the scarf and held her hair back from her cheek.

Apart from a slight intake of his breath Aaron scarcely batted an eyelid. 'I've known all about it, right from the start,' he told her. 'Maggie kept me informed. But you're right, Jo,' his fingers took hold of her chin, turning her face around to the light, 'it doesn't matter. There's make-up to hide it on stage and camera angles in advertising.'

Jo frowned and shrugged.

'Jo? Don't you realise what I'm saying? I can have you back on the stage, at the top, just like that.' He snapped his fingers. 'And you can pick and choose which particular product you want to do in television advertising. After the success of that last campaign you can name your own price.'

'Oh, Aaron, thanks for that vote of confidence, but no, thanks,' Jo sighed. 'I've been off the scene for too long.'

'Rot, Jo! And you know it. Look, Jo,' he leant across and picked up her hand, 'I don't think you realise just how much you've been missed.'

Jo gave him a sceptical look and Aaron shook his head in mild exasperation.

'In our world, Jo, pretty faces come and go—mostly go. But you've got what all of those pretty faces would trade their beauty for, love—talent. Talent is the only ageless commodity. You've got enough talent for three with some left over.'

'Aaron——' Jo began, but he interrupted her.

'No, Jo, let me finish. There's this play I'll be directing and I'd like you to take the female lead. I've got a copy of the script in my car and I want to leave it with you so you can read it.'

Jo shook her head. 'I'm sorry, Aaron, I don't want to get back into that world again,' she said flatly.

Aaron looked about to argue with her, but he sighed instead and shrugged his shoulders. 'Well, I tried. But I guess it's your decision.' He sipped his coffee. 'What are your plans, then? I mean, what are you going to do when the housekeeper comes back? What happens at the end of this temporary job?'

'I haven't really thought about it,' Jo said evenly. 'I may stay down here. In Maggie's cottage, I mean.' She didn't meet his eyes, knowing as she said it that that would be the last thing she could do. To be so close to Jake and yet so far away would be too much for her to bear.

'You mean you're going to vegetate down here like a hermit when you've got talent to burn,' Aaron bit out, an edge of anger entering his voice.

'I like ... I like the solitude,' Jo said lamely. If Aaron only knew the half of it! If Jake wanted her to stay here, if Jake ... Jo pulled herself up, reminding herself harshly that there were no 'ifs' when it came to Jake and herself.

'Humph!' Aaron frowned down at his hands. 'What's the fellow you're working for like?'

Aaron's words startled Jo, on top of her own anguish-filled thoughts.

'I take it he's the little girl's uncle?' Aaron drained his coffee cup.

'He's a writer,' Jo answered reluctantly.

'Oh. A would-like-to-be or a successful one?'

'Pretty successful.'

'Do I know him?' Aaron watched her closely as she hesitated before answering.

'I'm not sure whether he would care to have everyone know where he's living,' Jo began, and Aaron raised his eyebrows.

'Just how famous is he? Come on, Jo, I'm dying of curiosity?' he appealed to her. 'You know I won't let it go any farther. My lips are sealed.' He pinched his lips together with his fingers.

Jo smiled faintly. 'All right—Jason Marsh.'

Aaron sat up and gave a low whistle. '*The* Jason Marsh? Wow! I see what you mean. He's known to guard his privacy with the same determination that the Yanks guard Fort Knox.' He gave Jo another piercing look. 'I met him last year at a publishers' do down in Sydney. He's not a bad sort of bloke.' He paused and watched her carefully. 'Nice-looking, or at least he must have had something, because all the females present were falling all over him. What's the latest in-word, macho?'

'Yes, I suppose he is rather attractive.' Jo's throat threatened to close and when Aaron remained silent she looked up to find his eyes resting thoughtfully on her and she blushed.

'Ah,' he said softly, 'I see. Is he the reason why you're not interested in resuming your career?'

'Of course not. It's not like that, Aaron. Jake . . . he . . . It's not like that,' she finished lamely, not even sounding convincing to her own ears. 'He's engaged,' she added flatly.

Aaron continued to watch her and then raised his

hands expressively, not pursuing that subject. 'Then why not read the script?'

'I just don't want to, Aaron. It would be a waste of time.' Jo took a deep breath. 'Perhaps I'm like someone who's fallen off a horse. I didn't get straight back into the saddle and now I've lost my nerve.'

Aaron gave a laugh of disbelief.

'I suppose I don't have the motivation to find my nerve again,' Jo said expressionlessly.

'It's a wicked waste, girl, if you but knew it.' Aaron shook his head regretfully. 'And I was so sure I could talk you around with my fatal persuasive charm,' he grinned crookedly.

Jo smiled at him. 'I'm truly sorry, Aaron.'

'Not as sorry as I am, believe me,' he said, his eyes resting on her intensely, and Jo blushed again.

'I . . . I didn't thank you . . . for the flowers and the good wishes when I . . . was in hospital. I appreciated it, Aaron.' She swallowed a lump in her throat. 'And I'm sorry I didn't see you. I wasn't in any fit state emotionally to face anyone.'

'That's okay and understandable. It was a pretty harrowing time for you.'

'Yes,' Jo said softly. 'How are your parents?'

'Fine.' Aaron followed her lead into a change of subject and they chatted amicably for nearly an hour before he reluctantly ro se to take his leave.

'I promised the friends I'm staying with that I'd be back for dinner,' he said as Jo and Sam walked with him to his car. Opening the door, he reached inside and took a thick brown envelope from the front seat and thrust it into Jo's hands. 'Take it and read it, Jo. For me.'

'Aaron, I . . . .'

'Just read it. Where's the harm?' he asked. 'I've scrawled my phone number on the packet so you can get in touch with me if you want to. I wish you would anyway.'

Jo laughed exasperatedly. 'You are very persistent, Aaron Daniel,' she said with mock exasperation.

He smiled back and leaned down to kiss her gently on the forehead before climbing into the car.

Once Sam was settled to sleep that night Jo went to her room, not sure of the time Jake and Lexie would be returning and determined not to have either of them think she was waiting up for them. She looked at Aaron's script a couple of times before curiosity overcame her and against her better judgment she took the script out of its envelope and began to read.

Time passed as she lost herself in the play, and it was well after midnight when she reached the end. Aaron was right, it was a brilliant piece of writing, and back then she would have given her eye-teeth for the female lead. Now it didn't hold the same magic for her, no thrill of a burning urge to create, no thirst to take the typewritten words and give them life. The vital spark had died and she had no desire to rekindle it.

Flicking off her reading lamp, Jo lay back in the darkness, her eyelids drooping tiredly. Maybe she should take Aaron's advice and go back. No! screamed a voice inside her. There could be no going back. But she could move on. It would be a perfect excuse to leave, to turn her back on her foolishness over Jake Marshall, and to begin a new life.

Her lips twisted with a touch of the same old cynicism. Wasn't that what everyone had suggested she do, that she should begin a new life, that she should be starting over? Oh, Jake, her heart cried out. Why couldn't it have been with you?

Understandably Jo was feeling decidedly jaded as she prepared Sam's breakfast next morning. Jake's car was drawn up outside and although Jo hadn't heard their return it must have been near enough to dawn when they arrived home. When Jake walked into the kitchen, dressed in casual slacks and knit shirt, both Jo and Sam looked up in surprise.

'Hi, Uncle Jake! We thought you'd still be asleep. Did you have a good time at your party?'

Smiling at his niece, Jake sat down at the table. After one quick glance Jo decided he looked as tired as she felt. 'Not bad,' he replied. 'How about you? Did you and Jo go down on to the beach?' he asked, nodding his thanks to Jo as she set a cup of coffee in front of him. He took a mouthful and sighed appreciatively.

'No,' Sam shook her head. 'We did some gardening and we had afternoon tea with Aaron.'

Jake halted in the middle of lifting his cup to his mouth and raised an eyebrow at his niece.

'Aaron's Jo's friend,' Sam explained. 'I like him. He's nice 'cause he smiles a lot. And,' Sam giggled, covering her mouth with a small hand, 'he kissed her goodbye.'

Jake's eyes moved to Jo and his face seemed to have set in a cold tenseness.

'He . . . he was a friend . . . is a friend of mine,' Jo stammered, an unjustified guilt stilting her words, and she chastised herself angrily. Why should she feel guilty? 'I worked with him and I've known him for quite a few years. Would you like bacon and eggs for breakfast?'

Jake's eyes remained on her for a few moments before he shook his head. 'This coffee will do.'

Jo sat down at the table to finish her toast and tea while Sam chatted on innocently about their garden, unaware of the thick tension between the two adults. After drinking his coffee Jake disappeared into his study and with Lexie still in her room Jo began to tidy up the living-room, moving around quietly so as not to disturb either Lexie or Jake. She had sent Sam outside to play and she was lost in her own thoughts when she heard the study door open and she turned to find Jake leaning in the doorway watching her, his eyes dark and hostile.

Taking a steadying breath, Jo turned back to finish straightening the cushions on the lounge chair conscious of the quickened thumping of her heartbeats in her ears.

'Who was this fellow?' he asked at last, and Jo turned back to him, a cushion clutched defensively in her arms. He had moved into the room and stood a few feet from her, his relaxed-looking stance with hands on his hips not deceiving Jo in the slightest. He was as taut as a coiled spring and she took an involuntary step backwards, her legs coming up against the lounge chair.

'Well, who was he?' he repeated.

'Just who I said, a friend I used to work with!' Jo replied, her voice a shade higher in her nervousness.

'How did he know you were here?' Jake hadn't moved a millimetre, his eyes bored into her.

'He . . . my sister . . .' Jo stammered, and gulped a breath. 'Actually he found out from my sister's children. Maggie wouldn't have told him.'

'Then you didn't want him to know where you were?'

'Yes—no. Not exactly.'

'Yes—no. Not exactly,' Jake repeated sarcastically. 'That about covers the lot.'

'I . . . I meant I didn't care to see anyone from the time of the . . . the accident, not that I didn't want to see Aaron personally,' Jo tried to explain.

'But you still invited him in.'

Jo shrugged. 'He'd come all this way and when I saw him I . . .' she paused. 'I was just being sociable.'

'Sociable?' His voice was ominously quiet. 'You didn't want to see him, but you were being sociable.

And were you still being sociable when you let him kiss you?'

'It wasn't like that.' Jo looked up at him levelly.

'Like what?'

'Like you're implying.'

'Guilty conscience, Jo?' he sneered.

'No, I haven't.' She raised her voice in indignation and turned aside from him, throwing the cushion back on to the chair as she went to walk away from him.

His strong fingers grabbed her arm and swung her none too gently back to face him. 'Let's have the truth, Jo!'

'I have told you the truth,' she bit out angrily.

'Have you? Let me make a guess.' Only inches separated their bodies as he glared ruthlessly down at her. 'You and this Aaron had a lovers' tiff and you took yourself off down here to bring him back into line knowing he'd find out where you were from your family and come running after you.'

'No! That's perfectly ridiculous!' Jo stared up at him incredulously. 'How could you say that? Aaron and I are friends. He ... he was a friend of my husband's.'

Jake's lips compressed tightly. 'That means little or nothing to anyone these days,' he said suggestively. 'Sounds like just one big happy family to me.'

'Jake, please, stop this,' Jo pleaded, trying to break out of his vice-like grip. 'It's simply not true. Aaron came to see me to offer me a part in a play he's directing.'

Jake's eyes searched her face. 'He's a director?'

Jo nodded. 'Actually, you may not remember him, but he said he met you in Sydney. Aaron Daniel.'

'You told him who I was?' His hand tightened again on her arm biting painfully into her flesh.

'I told him in confidence. He won't pass it on.'

'I only have your word for that,' he ground out.

'Yes, you do.' Jo struggled against him. 'Let me go, Jake, you're hurting me!'

'Hurting you?' he muttered angrily under his breath. 'I could shake the life out of you!' His fingers tightened and he thrust her from him, turning away from her, his hand rubbing the back of his neck.

'When will you be starting rehearsals?' he asked flatly.

'Rehearsals?' Jo repeated blankly, her fingers massaging the bruises Jake's fingers had left.

'For this play,' he said shortly. 'I'll have to get someone to look after Sam.'

Here was her chance to get out, to leave with dignity, before she let him see how much she loved him, how hard she had fallen, how . . . But suddenly she couldn't take it.

'I said I'd stay until Chrissie was well enough to return,' she began.

'Look, Jo,' he spun around to face her, 'I wouldn't expect anyone to keep me to such an arrangement when it meant a chance to pick up the threads of my career again, so I wouldn't ask it of you. You were a brilliant actress with a brilliant future. Your carer was interrupted, and now where's your chance to continue on with it.'

'You want me to take the part?' Jo asked quietly, everything forgotten, Lexie, Aaron, as a steady ache washed over her entire body. I don't want to take the part, she screamed inside herself. I just want to be with you. I want your love and your . . . Don't think! Don't think! She bit her lip before she could cast her pride aside and let the words escape from her heart.

'It's not a case of what I want or don't want.' He strode over to the window and rested his hands on the sill and the silence that followed his words shrieked loudly. Then he straightened and looked across the room, his eyes resting broodingly on her. 'I'll see some employment agencies when I take Lexie back to the city this afternoon, if you wouldn't mind staying on until I find a replacement.'

CHAPTER TEN

IMMEDIATELY after lunch Jake and Lexie set off for the city, and with Jake's departure a cloud of downheartedness seemed to settle about Jo. Even the little girl's chatter couldn't dispel her sadness, but at least Sam's presence forced her into making the effort to keep the depression at bay.

Until that morning when Jake had advised her to consider Aaron's offer of a part in his play she knew that deep down she had been holding a faint hope that somehow she had not been mistaken, that Jake returned some of the feeling she felt for him. Now she realised how foolish she had been. It was so blatantly obvious that their lovemaking had meant nothing to Jake and that afterwards he might even have experienced some annoyance with himself for allowing it to happen. Jo cringed inside, feeling cheap and sordid, and her dejection deepened.

How brief had been her moment of happiness! Tears flooded her eyes. She had lost her self-respect in that one uncharacteristic moment when she had allowed the passion Jake aroused within her to take control.

Her self-chastisement did nothing to relieve her despondency and she wished she had someone to turn to, to confide in the way she used to confide in . . . Maggie! Just the sound of Maggie's voice would soothe her. Some of her stepsister's calm levelheadedness was exactly what she needed.

Jo reached for the telephone. There was no reason why she shouldn't go up to Brisbane to visit Maggie. Jake had said he would most probably be in the city for a couple of days, so she could take Sam with her. It would be a change for Sam as well to mix with two little girls of her own age. In no time at all Jo had arranged to spend the night with Maggie and Ben and then drive back to the coast the following afternoon.

With some positive action decided she felt better, and before they left she rang Jake's hotel, leaving a message for him telling him where she could be contacted if it was necessary. And then they were on their way.

'Do you think they'll like me, Jo?' Sam asked, subdued now Jo informed her that their destination was the rambling old house at the end of the street.

'Of course they will,' Jo reassured her gently as she turned into the driveway and switched off the engine.

She had barely done so when two little girls followed by a dark-haired young woman flew down the steps to reach the car almost before Jo could open her door.

'Jo, it seems like years, let alone weeks!' Maggie hugged her tightly before being forced to relinquish Jo to the hugs of the two little dark-haired replicas of their mother, both clamouring at once for Jo's attention.

'Hi there! Over your measles?' Jo hugged them in turn.

'I had spots everywhere,' Tracey told her, round-eyed.

'So did Daddy,' added Kerry, not to be outdone.

'I've brought someone with me I'd like you to meet.' Jo turned to help Sam out of the car, holding her hand as she hung shyly back. 'This is Sam, a friend of mine. Sam, meet Kerry and Tracey and my sister Maggie.'

'Hi!' they chorused.

'Would you like to see our new dolls' house?' asked Kerry. 'Daddy's built it in the back yard and it's a really house—you can walk inside and everything.'

'Go on, Sam,' Jo encouraged her gently.

'You won't leave without me, will you, Jo?' Sam asked solemnly.

'I won't, I promise.' Jo knelt down beside her and tucked her blouse into her shorts. 'We're staying the night, remember?'

Sam nodded, and the other two little girls bore her excitedly off around the side of the house.

Jo's eyes followed Sam for a moment and then she turned back to her sister. 'Oh, Maggie, it's good to see you!'

'You, too,' Maggie grinned back. 'You look gorgeous, all fit and suntanned. The sea air has done wonders.'

Jo collected their bags from the back of the car and followed Maggie inside. 'You're sure you don't mind us turning up at such short notice? I mean, you and Ben hadn't planned on going out or anything?'

'Don't be daft. You know you can come any time,' Maggie reassured her. 'As a matter of fact, Ben's working late tonight, so we can natter away to our hearts' content. He won't be home till one at least. I've put a stretcher into your old room for the little girl in case she felt a bit upset in a strange house, so it's all organised.'

'Thanks, Maggie,' Jo said sincerely as she put their cases in her room, her eyes moving over the familiar four walls. It seemed an age since she had left, so much had happened in so short a time.

'Let's have a cuppa,' Maggie interrupted her thoughts. 'The kids can have half an hour playing outside before it begins to get dark, so you can tell me all. I've been dying to get down to see you, but with Ben doing all this overtime on top of the measles it's been well nigh impossible.' She plugged in the electric kettle while Jo set out the cups and saucers. 'Did you have a good run up here?'

'Mmm, pretty good. It's a long trip, though.' Jo flexed her tired muscles.

'You know, apart from looking terrific with your tan, you do look a little tired.' Maggie set the teapot on the table and sat down opposite Jo, giving her a thorough scrutiny. 'Are you still not sleeping, love?'

'Oh, on and off.' Jo sighed unconsciously.

'Okay, Jo, out with it,' Maggie prompted. 'What's the trouble? I guessed there was something by your voice on the phone this afternoon.'

'Oh, Maggie, you must be sick and tired of me. Just when you thought you were well rid of me here I turn up again to cry on your shoulder.' Jo brushed the tears from her eyes.

'Rubbish! What are sisters for? You'd do the same for me, love.'

Jo smiled tearfully. 'Except that you're far too sensible to let yourself fall apart the way I did.'

'You could hardly be blamed for that, Jo.' Maggie patted Jo's hand sympathetically. 'Put under the strain that you were subjected to anyone would have cracked up. Is it . . . Is it any easier now?' she asked quietly. 'I mean, did the cottage do any good?'

'Yes,' Jo nodded. 'I think I'm much more at peace with it, maybe as much as I'll ever be, anyway.'

Maggie gave her a level look. 'So why the sleepless nights?'

Jo shrugged, needing desperately to confide in Maggie but not knowing where to start, and she absently ran her hand over her cheek, following the furrow of the scar.

'Jo, you're not—well, worrying about that, are you?' Maggie's eyes indicated Jo's scarred cheek.

'No, Maggie. I rarely think about it now.' Jo laughed humourlessly. 'Funny how the passing of time can change our priorities. When I went down to the cottage my face was playing on my mind every other moment of the day and night, along with . . .' She paused. 'I was so wrapped up in myself I don't know why you and Ben put up with me all those months.'

'We love you, Jo, and we knew you'd come out of it in time.' Maggie said simply. 'No one could blame you.'

'I could have wallowed in self-pity for the rest of my life, because that's what I planned to do. I . . . I lied to you about going down to the cottage to write. I just wanted to drift and brood over how cruel life had been to me. It took Sam to start me out of it.'

Maggie raised her eyebrows.

'When I first saw her on the beach I felt so angry and defensive. But she was such a . . . trusting little thing and I couldn't take my own aggression out on her, although I very nearly did in the beginning. Then Chrissie, the Marshalls' housekeeper, told me how Sam's parents were killed virtually before her eyes, and I realised I wasn't the only person to have lost my family so tragically. Sam was just a child, even less capable of coping with the whole thing than I was. It gave me more to think about than my own selfish self,' Jo finished candidly.

'Jo! Jo!' Sam came running inside with Maggie's girls. 'Can I get my doll out of the car?'

'I brought it inside with our bags,' Jo told her. 'Tracey will show you which room.'

'Okay.' She went to hurry off, but stopped and turned excitedly back to Jo. 'You should see the dolls' house, Jo. It's beautiful! I wish we could show Uncle Jake.'

'And talking about Uncle Jake,' Maggie remarked when the children had left them, 'what's he like? Tall, dark and handsome, didn't you say?'

Jo blushed. 'I suppose that about describes him.'

'And is this Jake Marshall responsible for the dark circles under your eyes?' Maggie adroitly went straight to the heart of Jo's problem.

Unable to prevent her eyes from welling with tears,

Jo shook her head dejectedly. 'Is it so obvious?'

'Only to me, maybe. But I did have a slight suspicion when you phoned to tell me you were going over there. Your voice changed when you talked about him, or rather didn't talk about him. You became very offhand to the point of understatement.' Maggie grinned. 'So if he's tall, dark and handsome, what's the problem?'

'Everything! Maggie, I've been the stupidest, blindest, most foolish . . .'

'Flattering, I must say!' quipped Maggie, the sympathy in her tone softening her teasing words. 'You must be in love with the man.'

'It's happened so quickly I didn't even realise . . . Oh, Maggie, I love him so much. But he . . .' Jo swallowed. 'He . . .'

'Doesn't feel the same way,' finished Maggie, and Jo nodded. 'Did he say that?' Maggie asked.

'Not exactly. We haven't—well, discussed it.'

'Then I don't see the problem. If you want him, love, all you need to do is flutter those big blue eyes at him and I can't see any red-blooded guy resisting.' Maggie gave her a wink.

'I wish it was that simple,' Jo sighed. 'I mean, I've never felt this way about anyone before. Even Mike,' she added in a whisper. 'Jake only has to look at me and I can't . . .' She stopped, the colour rising in her cheeks, and she looked down at the cup in her hands. 'He's engaged to be married,' she said flatly.

'Engaged?' Maggie repeated. 'I see,' she said seriously. 'I'm sorry, love.'

Jo nodded and they were silent for a few moments, each lost in her own thoughts.

'What will you do?' Maggie asked at last.

'Leave. That's all I can do,' Jo replied. 'Jake's in Brisbane at the moment getting someone else to look after Sam.'

'You mean he asked you to leave?'

'No. He . . . he thinks I'll be going back into acting. You see, Aaron turned up and offered me this part . . .'

'Aaron Daniel? How on earth did he find you?' asked Maggie. 'He was here last week, but he didn't mention he'd be seeing you and he was asking after you, too.'

'He said the girls told him where I was.'

'Tracey and Kerry? You mean he pumped them? My God, he's got some nerve! Oh, Jo, I'm sorry. I never even thought to warn the kids.' Maggie looked concerned.

'It's all right,' Jo reassured her. 'We had a good chat and he insisted I read his play hoping I'd decide to take one of the parts.'

'And will you?'

'I may do. At least it will give me an excuse to leave and save my dignity. For what it's worth,' she added self-derisively. 'I guess I'll have to do something.'

Maggie nodded. 'What about Aaron? I always felt that you'd only have to give him a little encouragement and he'd fall at your feet.'

'We're just friends, Maggie. I don't think I could settle for that, not after knowing how it can be.'

'I guess not,' Maggie sighed, and stood up. 'Well, it's starting to get dark. Let's go out and inspect the dolls' house and then we'll see about dinner.'

A few hours spent with her sister did much to console Jo, and although the ache of longing for Jake still filled her with a throbbing heaviness she was glad she had come. As she watched Sam thoroughly enjoying herself she knew a twinge of painful remorse that the little girl's world would be upset yet again. Chrissie would be returning soon, Jo told herself, so perhaps Sam would only miss her for a short time.

After dinner she rang Aaron to tell him she had read his play, but despite his pressures she refused to commit herself to accepting the role he offered, and it was almost eleven o'clock when a car turned into the driveway.

'Ben's early,' Maggie frowned. 'I wonder why he's leaving the car out,' she remarked as she went down the hallway to open the front door.

Listening to the soft strains of the record Maggie had switched on for her to hear, Jo sat relaxed in her chair, her head resting back, her eyes closed, trying to shut everything out of her mind. But Jake's face swam before her, his voice drifted deeply across her thoughts.

'Jo?' said Maggie from the doorway. 'There's someone to see you.'

Jo sat up, her body tensing as Maggie stood aside and Jake's tall, so very familiar figure stepped into the room. The living-room seemed to suddenly diminish in size and Jo paled, pushing herself shakily to her feet, completely robbed of the power of speech.

'Well,' Maggie exclaimed brightly, 'I'll leave you with Jo, Mr Marshall, while I go and make a cup of tea.'

As Maggie left Jo opened her mouth to call her back, but no words came and her eyes flew back to Jake as he took a couple of paces towards her.

'What ... what are you doing here?' she asked brokenly, her startled gaze registering the tiredness in the drawn lines of his face, the redness of his eyes.

'Is that all you can say?' he ground out with portentous quietness. 'Do you know what I was thinking while you sat here socialising? Do you know ...?' He drew a deep breath. 'The hell you do!' He muttered and in two quick strides he had reached her, his hands wrenching her against the rock wall of his chest, his lips crushing hers in a desperate punishing kiss. For all its harshness his kiss fanned the flame of Jo's senses into an all-consuming fire.

Slowly the timbre of that kiss altered, passion replacing anger, and when Jake finally raised his head they stood together, breathing ragged, staring into each other's eyes.

Jo began to tremble, shocked by the intensity of her response to him, and his arms tightened about her. He closed his eyes resting his lips against her forehead.

'Jo! Jo!' he moaned huskily. 'There hasn't been a single moment these past few days when I haven't wanted to hold you like this, kiss you till you cried for mercy, wanted you until it was an ache eating away inside me.'

'Please don't, Jake.' Jo pushed her hands against his chest, 'We shouldn't . . .'

'Where you're concerned I can't trust myself, I proved that the other night,' he whispered, his lips finding hers again, so disturbingly caressing that any resistance Jo might have put up died away as she responded to his sensual demands in complete surrender.

His hands slid up her arms to rest on either side of her head, his fingers in the softness of her hair. 'I'm taking you back with me, Jo, and I'm not letting you go for the rest of our lives. If you want to continue your career then we'll move into town, but whatever we decide we'll be together.'

'But Jake . . .' Jo began, drawing a sharp breath, her responses surging as his finger gently traced the outline of her lips.

'No, let me finish, Jo,' he said, his voice thick with barely curbed passion. 'When I arrived back at the house and you were gone leaving no message I thought I'd lose my sanity. In those first tortured minutes something died inside me.'

A shudder passed over his body. 'I tried to tell myself there had to be a logical explanation, that you wouldn't have gone far with Sam without contacting me. I tried your cottage, I rang Chrissie. And I was just about out of alternatives and fast losing control when it crossed my mind that you might have rung my hotel.'

'Oh, Jake, I'm sorry,' said Jo. 'I thought you'd go straight there after you and Lexie . . .' Her voice died away and a flash of pain passed over her face. She struggled to free herself, but Jake held her fast.

'Don't, Jo. Lexie means nothing to me,' he began.

'How can you say that, Jake?' she cried. 'She's your fiancée. We have no right . . .'

'Lexie isn't and never has been my fiancée,' he said distinctly.

'But you said . . .'

'I know what I said.' He stood away from her running his hand through his hair. 'And I regretted it the moment I allowed you to believe it. I was so clever. I saw the little subterfuge as an effective screen, because you were getting to me, Jo, in a way no woman ever had before, and I admit at the time I wasn't overjoyed about it. I wasn't interested in anything permanent, I never had been. It was always a brief and mutually pleasurable interlude and then goodbye.'

Jo's eyes fell to her hands clutched in front of her, not daring to allow herself to think about where this moment was leading, wanting and rejecting at the same time.

'All that was before you came along,' he said huskily. 'That morning on the beach, when I behaved so abominably, the feel of you in my arms, that's when it began for me.' He put his finger beneath her chin, lifting her face until her eyes met his and her breath caught in her throat at the expression that smouldered in his eyes.

Deliberately his gaze moved to the scar on her cheek and he gently ran one finger down its jagged edge in much the same way that Sam had done not so very long ago, and Jo's eyes filled with tears.

'Forgive me for my brutish behaviour that morning,' he asked quietly. 'If it's any consolation I couldn't find enough words with which to reprimand myself. I'd as soon cut off my hand as hurt you like that again.'

'Please don't, Jake,' Jo swallowed the lump in her throat. 'You weren't to know.'

'That's beside the point. If I hadn't been so sure you were out to harm Sam I might have realised that you were running from me in fright rather than guilt.' He wiped away the tears on her cheeks with his thumb. 'For days afterwards I carried your scarf about with me, feeling you in my arms, catching the scent of your perfume, your hair. I couldn't have not sought you out again if my life depended on it.' His hand cupped the back of her head, cradling her against his shoulder. 'I love you, Jo, and I want to marry you. I'll do everything in my power to make you happy.'

'Oh, Jake!' Jo slipped her arms around his waist, turning her face into his chest.

'I'm not saying it will all be plain sailing, I can be a bear at times when I'm writing, but I know it can be good between us.' His fingers moved through her hair, savouring its softness. 'What do you say?' He held her from him, the smile in his eyes fading at the expression on her face. 'Jo?'

'Well, here's the tea.' Maggie breezed in, setting the tray on the coffee table, smiling from Jake to Jo, seemingly oblivious of the tension that had suddenly filled the air before she entered. 'I'm Jo's sister, by the way.' She held out her hand. 'Jo's told me quite a bit about you, Jake.'

'She has?' Jake cast a measured glance at Jo, who sank down into her chair before her trembling legs gave way completely.

'Yes. Ben, my husband, is an avid reader of your novels,' Maggie beamed at him. 'Black or white?' she asked easily as she began pouring the tea, Jake's set features not disconcerting her in the least.

Jo sat holding her cup, unable to even attempt to swallow the hot liquid, until eventually Maggie yawned rather theatrically and winked aside at her.

'Oh, dear, I am tired. I think I might call it a night. I hope you'll excuse me, Jake?' she smiled at him.

'Of course.' Jake set his almost untouched cup back on the table and stood up politely.

'I'll leave you two to continue your discussion. If you'd care to stay the night Jo can show you the spare divan in the sleep-out, you're quite welcome.' Maggie walked to the door and turned back to them. 'Pleased to meet you, Jake. Goodnight. 'Night, Jo.'

With Maggie's departure there was a heavy silence until Jake moved to stand in front of Jo's chair.

'Well, Jo?' he asked without expression.

'Well, what?' Jo swallowed, beginning to quiver inside, wishing Maggie was still with them to postpone the next few minutes. Her head was spinning with a thousand torturing thoughts. How she yearned to throw herself into the safety of his arms and tell him she had been longing for him to want her, need her, love her. But there was too much left unsaid, too many memories inhibiting her, and she sat in her chair with her hands clutched together, her eyes not meeting his.

'Jo, I asked you to be my wife,' he said evenly. 'Just a simple yes or no will do. That isn't too much to expect, is it?'

She shot a quick glance at him, her heart lurching at the sight of his even more haggard face, the tension that had seized his tired body. 'I'm sorry. I . . . It's not that simple, Jake.' Her voice was little more than a whisper.

He leant down, his hands firmly clasping her shoulders to draw her to her feet, his eyes holding hers intensely. 'I would have thought it would have been. You either want to marry me or you don't.' His fingers tightened a little. 'If you don't want to just say so.'

'It's not that I don't want to, it's just that I ... I can't.'

'Jo,' his voice sounded forced, 'no matter how much you loved your husband you can't bring him back.'

Jo stared up at him, a wave of familiar guilt taking hold of her, and although she opened her mouth to speak no sound came.

A flicker of pain crossed Jake's face and a pulse began to beat in his tensed jaw. Of its own volition, Jo's hand went up to touch him, sliding soothingly over the side of his face, her heart aching for him.

'No, Jake, Please, it's not that. We ... I ... Mike and I weren't in love,' she tried to explain. 'In the beginning perhaps—I don't know. I thought I loved him, but my feelings for him barely stood our first quarrel. Our marriage was a huge mistake.' Her voice faded away.

'Then why, Jo? For God's sake, I know you're not indifferent to me.' He drew a steadying breath. 'You mentioned a Jamie. Is it him?'

Jo's face paled. 'Jamie?' she whispered.

'Did you have an affair with him when your marriage began to go wrong?' Jake asked, and her eyes grew wide with bewilderment.

'An affair?' she repeated blankly. 'No. No, I thought you knew. You said you'd read the newspaper reports of the ... the accident.'

Jake frowned. 'I did. There was no mention of a Jamie.'

'Maybe there wouldn't have been,' Jo said almost to herself. 'I never allowed any publicity where Jamie ... where my son was concerned.'

Jake stared down at her, a little white about his mouth. 'Your son?' His eyes probed hers. 'He was in the car as well?'

Jo nodded, and seeing the pain in her eyes he wordlessly pulled her gently against him, resting his cheek against her head, holding her close.

'I couldn't go through it again, Jake,' Jo whispered flatly into the softness of his shirt. 'I couldn't have another child, suffer the agony of wondering if . . .'

'Jo, the whole of life is one big chance.' Jake held her away from him, his eyes not wavering from hers. 'If you don't take the chances then there's no point to any of it.'

'I can't, Jake. I love you too much to put it to the test. Don't you see? Everything I touch goes wrong— Mike, my marriage, and Jamie.' She brushed her hand across her eyes. 'Mostly Jamie.'

Jake sat down in a lounge chair and drew her on to his knee. 'I think you'd better tell me, Jo, from the beginning.'

And once she started to talk Jo couldn't stop. It was as though a dam inside her burst and the whole story poured out. At times she knew she wasn't being very clear, but Jake didn't interrupt. He simply let her talk and everything tumbled out. How she had met Mike, their whirlwind courtship and marriage. A thousand little things she scarcely knew she remembered, telling him even more than she had confided in Maggie. Only when she came to Jamie's birth did she falter, and she turned into Jake's arms, the pain too deep-seated for tears.

'He was so beautiful, Jake,' she said softly. 'And because Mike was so absolutely against my having him I felt he belonged only to me. That was so very wrong. I can see it now, but at the time . . .' tears spilled down her cheeks, 'I felt so guilty. A few weeks later they told me he was almost totally deaf. I couldn't help blaming myself. Mike wanted me to have an abortion and because I didn't Jamie . . . Oh, Jake, don't you see? I can't . . . What if . . .?'

'Jo, listen to me. There are any number of things

that can go wrong during any pregnancy,' he said evenly. 'There's no reason why it would happen again, but if it did we'd face it together. It's a chance we all take.'

'Jake, I don't think I'm strong enough to take that chance,' she said flatly.

'I'm strong enough for both of us,' he said huskily, his lips teasing her earlobe.

'Jake, please, I can't put that burden on you. And I can't think straight when you do that.'

'That's one of the reasons why I'm doing it. The way I see it, my love, you've been thinking far too much. From now on I'm going to keep you too busy to brood over anything. No matter what life dishes out, we're going to face it together, and we'll fly over the downs because the ups will make it so worthwhile.' His lips found hers with a firm gentleness that had her arms sliding around him as she responded with all the love that burned for him, and when they drew breathlessly apart he grinned crookedly down at her. 'What did I tell you, won't the ups be the best?'

Jo nodded. 'But, Jake, I'm afraid. I love you so much.'

He put his finger on her lips. 'From now on we concentrate on ups. I strictly forbid any unwarranted downs.' He kissed her almost reverently. 'This is our new beginning.'

Some time later Jo murmured sleepily in his arms, 'We should go to bed. Ben will be home soon and if Sam wakes up and I'm not there she may be frightened.'

'Mmm.' Jake nuzzled her earlobe. 'I can see between you and Sam I'm going to have to get used to getting less sleep.'

'Jake!' she blushed, her arms sliding around his neck.

'Well, you are going to marry me, aren't you?' he

asked teasingly, although his eyes watched her carefully.

Jo nodded, and he expelled the breath he had been
holding and raised her hand to his lips, kissing her
palm.

'Good. That should set everybody's mind at rest,
seeing that you got me into such a compromising situation,' he said with mock seriousness.

'I did?'

'Yes. Unchaperoned, too!'

'Sam was there,' Jo said indignantly, 'and besides,
nobody knew.'

'We knew.'

Jo laughed and he smiled back at her with satisfaction.

'I hope this will be all right with Sam,' Jo said.

'There won't be any problems there,' he said easily.
'Sam already thinks the world of you. She's been
dropping broad hints about your wifely attributes ever
since she first met you. I don't know why I was so
slow to look into her suggestion.' He stifled a yawn
and Jo moved contritely.

'You must be absolutely exhausted. We'd better go
to bed.' Jo tried to struggle off his lap.

Jake held her to him, his eyes dancing teasingly.
'What a thing to say!'

'You know what I mean,' she blushed.

'I surely do,' he murmured huskily as he got reluctantly to his feet, setting her down, to hold her lightly
in the circle of his arms.

She looked shyly up at him. 'What made you so sure
I'd marry you? I mean, was I so transparent about
how I felt about you?'

'You were never that. Not until you had that nightmare, anyway.' Jake closed his eyes. 'My God, I still
don't know how I made it through that night, holding you and not . . . until the morning, that was.' The

corners of his mouth lifted attractively.

'Afterwards I thought you were just taking advantage of an available moment.' Jo ran her finger along his slightly beard-roughened jaw.

'The very best available moment of my life. I'd reached the limit of my endurance by then. I had to get up and leave you or stay and make love to you. Then you gave me that sleepy smile and the decision was taken out of my hands. When you told me you loved me . . .'

'When I what?' Jo exclaimed.

'Those words were the sweetest music I've ever heard,' he said seriously.

'Then I did tell you? When I woke up and you'd gone I wasn't sure if I had actually said it. I was thinking it and . . .' Jo sobered. 'You were so distant. I didn't know what to think.'

'I went because I didn't want you to be embarrassed if Sam bounded in with awkward questions.' Jake shook his head. 'Everytime I tried to talk to you later Sam was there, and by the time Lexie turned up I was about to commit blue murder! And knowing Lexie as I do I couldn't let her see I didn't want her there or she'd have stayed for a month. They were the longest couple of days of my life.'

'Lexie implied . . .' Jo began, and swallowed, her eyes on the collar of his shirt. 'Well, were you and she . . .'

'No. We were just friends, no more,' he said lightly.

'She said you . . . she mentioned Sam's mother.' Jo's eyes met his and he sobered.

'Lexie has been busy!' He sighed. 'I met Denise when I was still at university and I fell for her. She seemed to feel the same about me until she met my older brother. It was love at first sight for both of them and they married pretty well straight away, something neither of them ever regretted. My pride took a bashing,' he smiled crookedly, 'but I was soon over it. I never blamed either of them for it, Jo, although I don't agree with the way they left Sam with Denise's mother so much. But,' he shrugged, 'it was their decision.'

Jo smiled up at him. 'It may please you to know I was green with jealousy.'

'I know the feeling. When Sam told me so innocently about that Daniel guy kissing you goodbye, for a moment I couldn't trust myself to look at you.' His eyes held hers. 'What about that, Jo? Do you want to go back into stage work?'

Jo shook her head without reservation. 'No. Even before the accident I'd lost my motivation in that direction. I want to be with you and Sam.'

His lips gently found hers and they leaned sleepily together.

Jake sighed. 'Well, where's this divan your sister offered me?' he asked with a grimace. 'I don't suppose it's big enough for two?'

'No.' Jo shook her head.

'No.' He groaned regretfully, a promise burning in his eyes.

Drowsily Jo settled back in her bed listening to Sam's even breathing, and smiled contentedly, her fingers touching her lips still slightly swollen from Jake's kisses. Her heart swelled with unshadowed happiness.

Jake was right. She had to take this chance or she would have no life at all, for to go on without Jake would be just that, no life at all.

Her lips curved into a smile again. Tomorrow would be the beginning. She would be starting over. With Jake.

Harlequin® Plus

A WORD ABOUT THE AUTHOR

Australian author Lynsey Stevens has a quality that everyone loves in a person, and few can resist in a writer: a sense of humor. Of herself, she cheerfully says, "Although I'm not an oil painting, I make up for it by being 'a very nice person' with a scintillating personality."

Lynsey's days are spent at a job she thoroughly enjoys. She is a librarian who engages in all sorts of professional activities related to books, though her first love is her writing.

She began with attempts at historical romance, progressed to adventure and espionage and even tried her hand at what she calls "sexy stories" – from which she claims to have gained her expertise at the "steamy" scenes in her present books.

Her first romance novel was not as readily accepted for publication as she had expected – in fact, it was rejected. But undaunted, spunky Lynsey kept at it, and she now has several published books to her credit.

As to real-life romance, she hints at the presence of a Harlequin hero in her life, but swears he's just a good friend – though she does admit she's not the type to kiss and tell under any circumstances!

Harlequin reaches
into the hearts and minds
of women across America
to bring you

Harlequin
American Romance™

Enter a uniquely exciting
new world with

Harlequin
American Romance™

Harlequin American Romances are the first romances to explore today's love relationships. These compelling novels reach into the hearts and minds of women across America... probing the most intimate moments of romance, love and desire.

You'll follow romantic heroines and irresistible men as they boldly face confusing choices. Career first, love later? Love without marriage? Long-distance relationships? All the experiences that make love real are captured in the tender, loving pages of **Harlequin American Romances.**

What makes American women so different when it comes to love? Find out with **Harlequin American Romance!**

Send for your introductory FREE book now!

Get this book FREE!

Mail to:

Harlequin Reader Service

In the U.S.
2504 West Southern Avenue
Tempe, AZ 85282

In Canada
649 Ontario Street
Stratford, Ontario N5A 6W2

YES! I want to be one of the first to discover **Harlequin American Romance.** Send me FREE and without obligation *Twice in a Lifetime.* If you do not hear from me after I have examined my FREE book, please send me the 4 new **Harlequin American Romances** each month as soon as they come off the presses. I understand that I will be billed only $2.25 for each book (total $9.00). There are no shipping or handling charges. There is no minimum number of books that I have to purchase. In fact, I may cancel this arrangement at any time. *Twice in a Lifetime* is mine to keep as a FREE gift, even if I do not buy any additional books.

Name _____ (please print)

Address _____ Apt. no.

City _____ State/Prov. _____ Zip/Postal Code

Signature (If under 18, parent or guardian must sign.)